GROVER STATE

Also by T. C. Downer

Implied Emancipation
The Forum
Open Prison
The Man in the Yellow Shirt
The Last Stop
Riding the Rocket, Volume One: Westbound to Kipling
Riding the Rocket, Volume Two: Eastbound to Kennedy
The Human Experience: A Collection of Short Stories, Volume One

GROVER STATE

T. C. DOWNER

This book is a work of fiction. Names, characters,
places, and incidents either are products of the
author's imagination or are used fictitiously. Any
resemblance to actual persons, living or dead, events,
or locales is entirely coincidental.

T. C. Downer

For more information, visit www.tcdowner.com

ISBN-13 978-1-927943-16-8

To my wonderful family

Chapter 1

There were many things that I hated about Grover State, and my identity chip was one of them. As strong as my feelings were, I had to remember to keep them to myself. My parents, Amanda and Lucas, had warned me about displaying any act of aggression towards the state. It didn't help that every microscopic detail about me was tracked via my identity chip, including my current location and state of consciousness. Unfortunately, it wasn't a very good alarm clock.

I didn't hear my alarm, and was on the verge of being late for my education session. Quickly jumping out of bed, I ran into the Education Room without bothering to change out of my sleepwear. I did not want to start the day off with an infraction, before it even began.

I swung open the door to the Education Room, and slammed it behind me. As soon as the latch automatically clicked into place, which prevented students from leaving prior to the end of the lesson, my professor appeared.

I was assigned to Professor Kiln-Roberts. He was a high priority citizen. I could tell because he had two last names. Only high priority citizens were allowed to carry two last names. Mid and low priority citizens were only allowed one. I was always jealous that I wasn't placed in a high priority home, but at least I wasn't classified as low priority.

I mimicked the professor's movements, and placed my right hand above my heart. The lights dimmed, and he started reciting the Grover State Pledge. I joined him.

"I pledge my loyalty to Grover State, my keeper and protector. I am bound to serve, and do it gladly. Give me the strength to overcome the temptation of infractions, lest I be disciplined. I give myself to the state, knowing that I can never repay it back for all it has done for me. I am Grover State."

I hated having to recite the pledge every single day. If I could get away with it, I would not recite a single word. However, it wasn't worth getting an infraction for. The decibel level of my voice is continuously monitored by my identity chip, and I would automatically receive an infraction if it didn't register me reciting it.

As the lights turned back on, I refocused my

attention on the professor. Sometimes his image flickered in the light, and it made it hard for me to concentrate on what he was saying.

"Good morning, Megan Thomas. Shall we begin your lesson?" he asked, taking a seat at his teacher's podium. I didn't understand why he always insisted on sitting down. What was the point of being digitally projected if you stayed stationary for the majority of the time?

"Yes, professor," I answered.

"Please write a 1,000 word essay on the state's military. You will need to provide three ideas that could further secure our borders. You have until the end of your session to complete the paper. Failure to comply will result in an infraction."

"Yes, professor."

I disliked how he always threatened me with an infraction if I didn't do as he said. I always had to show respect to him, since he was classified as a higher priority citizen than me. If I was rude or disrespectful, that would cost me an infraction. If you received five infractions in any one given day, you had to submit yourself to re-education. Luckily, I have never gotten past four in one day.

I took a seat in the chair prominently

displayed in the middle of the room. A writing tray slid from an opening in the chair, and settled on top of my thighs. Opening the tray, I removed the writing tablet contained inside.

The writing tablet was a very simple device. Its only purpose was writing; you couldn't do anything else on it. A thin air board was digitally projected in front of me, and I started typing away.

The content of my essay was very dry. I had never been near the border, and didn't really care about the security surrounding them. I had a suspicion that border security was to keep us in, rather than keep whatever's out there out. However, that wasn't how we were supposed to think.

I typed as fast as I could, not having to care about spelling or grammar. The software used by the tablet automatically corrected spelling and grammar. Depending on how bad your grammar skills were, you could review your work and not even recognize what you wrote.

I chanced a few glances towards the professor, and saw him staring straight at me. It unnerved me, how he would always sit there watching me work, until I was done. I glanced back down at my tablet and continued writing.

As soon as my word count indicated that my essay was 1,003 words long, I quickly finished writing the paragraph I was in the middle of, and submitted the essay. I placed the writing tablet in the tray, and it slid back into the chair.

"I have completed the assignment, professor," I said.

"Very well, Megan Thomas. I will have your essay marked for tomorrow's session. Please view chapter six of your Arithmetic III text, and chapter eighteen of your Composition VI text. I shall see you tomorrow. Good day," he responded.

"Good day, professor."

His digital projection disappeared as quickly as it had appeared, and I was left alone in the room. After a few more seconds, the door to the Education Room automatically unlocked and slid open.

I wanted to leave the room, to seek refuge in my own, but I knew I'd be better off completing my assignments immediately. I walked over to the Educational Texts cabinet, and retrieved the two texts I was assigned.

The texts were imbedded in a small programmable chip. I removed it from its protective covering, and inserted it into my identity chip, which was located below my wrist on my left hand. As soon as my chip started to process the text, words started to appear before my eyes, feeding me the information.

After a little more than an hour, I had finished reading both assigned texts. I replaced the chips in their cabinet, and left the Education Room.

*****

I was getting bored. My parents usually arrived around this time, but they hadn't arrived home yet. I wasn't too worried about their safety or well-being. There was barely any crime in the state, and hardly anything bad ever happened.

My parents weren't biologically related to me. All children were produced by breeders, and then placed with people selected by the state to start a family.

There were six different life paths that you could potentially be assigned to. No one was able to choose their own, but there were rumours that high priority citizens were able to. I really wasn't looking forward to it, especially since I would be assigned to a path next year, on my sixteenth birthday.

The six life paths were elite, work, military, education, family, and breeder. As it most likely implies, the elite life path is only an option for high priority citizens. Those who were lucky enough to be assigned that path were given access to money beyond imagination, and were highly regarded in the state. I'm not too sure exactly what they did, besides indulge in their every wants and needs.

The work path was assigned to all classes of citizens. If you were a low priority citizen, you most likely ended up with a labour intensive job. Mid priority citizens usually occupied clerical and information processing jobs. High priority citizens were offered the best options: doctors, professors, politicians, and audio-visual performers.

If you were assigned to the military life path, you had to complete three more years of education. You had to cut all ties with your family and friends, and you remained on military property for the rest of your life, until you reached retirement. By that time, almost everyone you left behind was gone. This path was usually assigned to low priority citizens, but some mid priority citizens did get assigned.

The education path was only available to mid and high priority citizens. You continued your education with three years of university. During those three years, they would assess your skills and abilities to determine if you should be a professor or a researcher.

The family path is the life path that was currently assigned to my parents. Anyone except for those in the military path can apply for the family path. If they didn't have enough volunteers, they would assign it to couples. If there weren't enough suitable couples, they would pair two strangers together. Luckily for my parents, they applied and were accepted. They received me from the state, when I was six months old. All children must be released to a family before they turn one. The family path was the only one that could be jointly combined with another path, but it could be done alone as well.

If you were chosen to be a breeder, you were responsible for supplying the state with babies to provide to families. Only low priority citizens were selected for this life path. Both men and women had an equal chance of being selected, as the incubation sacs were surgically attached to your abdomen. They received one year off after each child was born, and were able to retire early, if they had produced ten children before the age of retirement.

The one universal constant between all life paths was that you automatically retired at 80 years of age. You were then granted access to your savings account, and could live however you wanted, as long as it was within the law of the state, and the confinements of your priority level.

Everyone received their paycheques daily via their identity chip, and the same deductions were taken from everyone. The state placed 10% of your pay to a mandatory savings account, which could only be accessed when you retired. They withheld 75% of your pay, to cover costs such as housing, medical services, transportation, and community services. The remaining 15% was credited to your account for your own personal use.

Everyone was assigned their life path at the age of 16. Luckily for me, I still had one year of freedom left, even if it didn't really feel all that free.

I decided to leave our unit, and walk around our housing block. As I left the unit, the door automatically shut behind me. I stared at the digital display above our unit number, and watched as it changed from 1 occupant to 0 occupants.

I was hoping that I would run into someone in the hallway. I didn't really have anywhere else to go. I had no friends, because everyone seemed like robotic replicas of each other. I didn't understand how people could be happy when they all acted the same.

After walking around the building twice and seeing no one, I decided to go sit outside. I sat down on the grass, and crossed my legs, tucking my feet under my knees. I enjoyed the fresh air, especially when it was quiet.

I had always wanted to see the sunset in person, but I've only ever been able to see it via broadcast. The state's curfew was one hour before sundown, until one hour after sunrise. Exceptions were made for those who had early morning jobs, and under other circumstances deemed appropriate by the state.

I've always wondered what it would be like to lay down on the cool grass, in the darkness of the night, looking up at the stars. I didn't really understand why we had a curfew, but there was nothing that could be done about it. Unless, of course, you were prepared to receive an infraction.

I uncrossed my legs as I lay down on the grass. The sun was shining brightly, causing me to squint. I closed my eyes, breathing in the fresh air.

"Hi Megan," said a voice above me.

Startled, I opened my eyes and raised myself to a seated position. I let out a breath as I realized who was standing above me. It was Rupert Guess, one of our neighbours.

Chapter 2

"Hi Rupert. You scared me. How are you?" I asked him, as he took a seat beside me on the grass.

"Not bad. I just got back from work. Are your parents home, by any chance?" he replied.

"No, I've been waiting for them for a while now. They're late."

"Ok," he said, as he got up from the grass. "Let's go inside, it's almost curfew."

I followed him inside the building, and we walked through the hallway. When we arrived at the door to my unit, I realized that I didn't want to be left alone.

"Do you want to come in to wait for my parents, since you were looking for them?" I asked Rupert.

He looked a little uneasy, and hesitated before replying, "Sure."

I stood in front of my unit door and scanned my identity chip on the reader below the unit number. The display turned green, and then the door slid open. I made my way towards the couch, and

Rupert followed behind me.

I wasn't sure why he was acting strange. He was usually very friendly, but today he seemed lost in his own thoughts.

"Did you take your vitamin today? You don't look well," I said.

"Huh? Oh, yes. I'm feeling a little under the weather."

"That's odd. I thought the vitamins were supposed to keep us from getting sick? Are you sure you didn't forget to take it?"

He ignored my question, and reclined back on the couch. I found it odd that he wasn't feeling well, since I've never once been sick in my entire life. The vitamins issued by the state improved our immune systems, and fed us the nutrients our bodies needed. I wasn't sure what was in it, but whatever it was worked.

I didn't know what else to say, so I just remained quiet. I was always intrigued by him, and I had so many questions I wanted to ask him. However, due to the constant surveillance we were under, I had no idea how I would go about asking him without being flagged and questioned by the police.

I knew that he was close to my parents, but they never went anywhere in public together. He worked at a grocery store near Housing Block M65. We lived in Housing Block M87, so it wasn't too much of a commute. Mom and dad sometimes bought their groceries from there, but I've never actually been to the store.

"I think I'm going to get going. If your parents come home tonight, please tell them that their order has been received at the store, and they can pick it up at their convenience," Rupert said.

"Oh, okay. Sure," I replied.

He got up and made his way to the door. I watched as he left, and the display changed to reflect 1 occupant. I felt sad that I was alone again, but I quickly got over it. What else could I do?

*****

I stayed up for a few more hours, but my parents still hadn't arrived. I wasn't worried, because I would have been alerted if anything happened to them. If they would have received an infraction, it would be indicated on the display near the door.

I was trying to figure out why they were out past the curfew. I couldn't think of a single reason why they would be granted an exception to the rule.

And even if they had been granted permission, surely they would have called to let me know.

I turned on the vision screen, and flipped through a couple stations. There were two national stations that everyone received, Grover State I and Grover State II. Grover State I was mostly just news. Grover State II showed live broadcasts around the city. Both stations were pretty boring, but everyone still spent most of their time watching them.

The other stations offered covered every topic imaginable. You just had to locate the station you wanted and add it to your line-up.

Last year, there was a case in the news about a group of people who managed to bypass the State Content Review Board, and made a channel available that broadcasts something that was previously banned. I wasn't sure what it was, since I never actually saw it, and all references to it was considered classified information. I knew that mom and dad must have seen it, but they never told me what it was about.

I continued flipping through stations, until I landed on one broadcasting animated shows. I let that play in the background as I slowly drifted into sleep.

Chapter 3

When I woke up, my neck and back were in pain. I had slept on the couch for the entire night. I knew that my parents weren't home, because they would have woken me up.

I looked everywhere for my parents, just to double check. I didn't find them anywhere, and their bed was neatly made. They hadn't come home last night.

Glancing down at my identity chip, I realized that my education session would begin in a few hours. I really didn't feel like going, but I had no choice. I didn't need to add the stress of receiving an infraction on top of everything else.

In the kitchen, I took out a breakfast pack and put it in the zapper. It only took one minute to fully cook my breakfast, which consisted of eggs, toasts, and sausages. Bringing my plate to the kitchen table, I sat down and ate.

Bringing the last bite to my mouth, I tried to keep myself calm. I was getting worried about my parents. They had never been away from the house for an entire night before. The display still showed that they had zero infractions, but that didn't help ease my mind.

Once I was in the Education Room, I wouldn't be able to leave until the session was over. Depending on the day, that could be anywhere from two to eight hours. I was never told beforehand how long the session would last.

Heading back into the living room, I noticed that the vision screen was still on from the night before. An animated show was playing, telling the story of a man who went around the state picking up litter. It was pretty boring. I changed the station over to Grover State I, deciding that any news must be more interesting than this.

The weather for the next couple of days was shown, and they talked about the latest group of citizens that just finished their re-education class. None of it really captured my attention, until they moved on to the next story.

The next story was about a car crash that happened last night. Car crashes were really rare, because not everyone was allowed to drive. Low priority citizens were trained and assigned as state drivers. If you needed to go anywhere, they would drive you. You were allowed unlimited transportation, to any destination you liked. The only exceptions were after curfew. They wouldn't bring you anywhere after curfew, unless you could prove that you had received an exemption.

They showed the footage of the accident. It happened on the Bay Creek bridge, only twenty minutes away from here. The video showed the car veering out of its lane, and hitting two other cars, before plunging into the water.

My attention was captivated. This was the first time I'd seen anything interesting on the vision screen for as long as I could remember.

"At this time, authorities have not released the cause of the accident. As you can see on the video, the driver veers off to the right, hitting two other vehicles before plunging into Bay Creek," the news reported said.

"The driver and both passengers occupying the car have been confirmed dead. At this time, none of the victims have been identified. Their identity chips have been damaged due to the acidity of the water. Experts are currently working on repairing the chips to identify the victims.

"Bay Creek has been cordoned off from the

public for the last twenty years, due to the acidity levels of the water. There is no direct access to the creek, except for a secured research site one kilometre from the water."

The screen changed from the reporter to an image of the accident. Three bodies were shown in blue bags; it was impossible to tell if they were male or female. The screen then changed to an image of the bodies, prior to them being placed in the bags. Upon seeing it displayed on the screen, my heart drop.

Staring back at me was the image of both of my parents. Their skin was pale white and wrinkled, and their eyes were closed. Their bodies were soaking wet, and their lips were blue. They were both dead.

*****

I was going through all my drawers, stuffing as much clothes as I could into my bag. Shirts, pants, underwear, bras, socks, pyjamas; everything went in there. I then went into the kitchen, and grabbed as much food as I could.

After the shock of seeing my dead parents on the vision screen, I realized something: I was now considered a Burden of the State. Once they managed to repair their identity chips and discovered who they were, they would come and find me.

Burdens of the State are any children under the age of sixteen who have lost both of their parents. Even if your parent's parents were still alive, you still became custody of the state. There was no way out of it, even if you were placed in a high priority family.

Once labelled, there was no escaping your fate. Burdens of the State were considered low priority citizens. The best you could hope for was to be placed in the military life path, as almost everyone looked down on them. It was almost a guarantee that you would never be able to attain the family path, unless your partner was assigned by the government.

Once a child entered the system under the title, they were placed in a work camp, where they were required to give up five hours of their time towards hard labour. The rest of the time was theirs to do with as they wished, but they weren't allowed to leave the grounds unless they were granted a special day pass.

I did not want to become a Burden of the State. As far as I was concerned, it was a fate worse than death. I was comfortable in my mid priority lifestyle, and I wasn't ready to give it up. There was no way I would become a low priority citizen.

Once my bag was packed, I headed to the front door, and left my unit. I ran through the hallway, glancing down at my chip: my education session would be starting in less than twenty minutes.

Outside, I ran as far as the sidewalk when I came to a dead stop. I couldn't run away. I couldn't escape my fate of being labelled a Burden of the State. They would know exactly where I would go, just as they knew exactly where I was right now. As long as I had my identity chip, there was no way to escape.

I turned around, and stared at my housing block. This might be one of the last times I see it. Sighing, I returned into my unit. Resigned to my fate, I walked into the Education Room with three minutes to spare.

*****

During the entire session, I wasn't able to concentrate on what Professor Kiln-Roberts was saying. He had handed me back the essay I had written yesterday, and was giving me feedback. I nodded in what I assumed to be appropriate places, and tried to convey an air of attention.

I was paranoid, thinking that the state police

would be waiting for me outside these doors, once the session had ended. I usually hoped that the session was short, so that I could leave the room as soon as possible. Today, I was hoping beyond hope that the class would last until the maximum allowable time.

After completing a few sheets of Arithmetic VI problems, he finally dismissed the session. Before disappearing, he gave me a listing of readings for tomorrow. I didn't hear what he said; it wouldn't matter anyways.

As soon as the door slid open, I ran out to the living room. I turned on the vision screen and changed it to Grover State I to watch the news. They ran another story on the accident, but there was no indication of whether or not they had managed to identify the bodies.

I started to relax myself when I heard rapid pounding on the front door of my unit. Startled, I got up and answered the door. Rupert was standing before me, out of breath.

Chapter 4

"Hi Megan, how are you today?" Rupert asked me, as he held onto the frame of the door.

"I'm fine. Are you okay?" I asked him.

There was sweat beading on his forehead, and his breathing was heavy.

"Yes, I'm great. Thanks for asking, Megan. Have you parents come home yet?"

I hesitated. I didn't know what to say. He knew that my parents were out past curfew last night. If I told him that they hadn't come home, he might realize that my parents were the ones that had died in the car accident.

"I think they both left for work before I woke up," I lied.

"Oh, that's unfortunate. Well then, I guess I could ask you for assistance. I brought your parents' order home for them. Would you mind coming to my unit to pick it up?"

"Sure, I guess."

I was a bit taken aback by the request, especially since it didn't add up to his current physical state. Nevertheless, I followed him. There was no reason for me to fear for my safety. Thanks to my identity chip, I had a personal body guard on duty twenty four hours a day.

I follow him into his unit, and sat down on the couch while he disappeared into another room. I assumed he was getting my parents' order, an order they would never receive.

I was actually quite curious as to what they had placed a special order for. For as long as I can remember, my parents had never special ordered any type of food.

I turned around as I heard Rupert coming back into the living room. He was holding a small black box.

"Do you mind holding this for a moment?" he asked me, as he sat down on the couch next to me.

"Sure," I replied, as I grabbed the small box from him. I tried to guess what it could contain, but I couldn't think of any food that was small enough to fit in there.

"What is it? My parents ordered this?" I asked him.

Ignoring my question, he produced another black box identical to the one I was holding from his pocket.

"Listen Megan, we don't have much time. You most likely know by now: your parents are dead. They died in a car accident. As of right now, they haven't been able to repair their identity chips, but it's only a matter of time until they do. You need to listen to me, and do as I say. Your parents asked me to protect you, if anything were to happen to them."

I was completely taken aback. At first I was shocked at what he was saying; I couldn't believe the words that were coming out of his mouth. Then I was shocked at what he was saying, because we were being monitored by our chips.

"Rupert, what's wrong with you? You're going to get us both in trouble. You're going to get my parents in trouble. You need some help; don't rope me into this," I said.

I got up from the couch and made my way towards the door. I already had enough on my plate. Being labelled a Burden of the State was bad enough; being labelled a traitor would be even worse.

Remembering the box in my hands, I turned around before I reached the door.

"What is this, anyways?" I asked. "Did my parents really order this from you?"

As I motioned to throw the box back towards him, he jumped off the couch and ran at me.

"Don't let go of the box, Megan! Don't let go!" he shouted.

I felt his hands envelop mine, as the edges of the box dug into my hand. We both wound up on the floor, and he continued addressing me.

"Listen, Megan. I know this is hard for you to hear. Before I say anything else, just promise me you won't let go of the box. That's a scrambler you're holding. It jams the signal from your identity chip: no information gets transmitted in or out as long as you are touching it.

"If you don't do exactly as I say, you will be detained by the state police, and subsequently labelled a Burden of the State. I promised your parents I wouldn't let that happen to you. We don't have much time to act. We're lucky if we have the rest of today before they find out your parent's identity.

"I will help you escape to our safe house, and I promise I will keep you safe. But before I can do that," he continued, "I need you to promise me that you will do as I say. I cannot risk you exposing our mission. You must promise."

I was in complete shock now. I didn't know

what to respond to him. How could I know if he was telling me the truth? What if he was a state police agent, and he was trying to con me into my own demise?

Not knowing what to say, I said the first thing that came into my mind: "Okay. Yes, I promise."

"Good," he said. "First things first, we're going to have to kill you."

Chapter 5

"What do you mean, you're going to have to kill me?"
I asked Rupert.

Rising from the floor, he helped me up and we
both sat down on the couch. Clutching the scrambler
close to my chest, I waited for him to answer me.

"We're going to need to fake your death.
Otherwise, the state police will be out looking for you
until they find you. And trust me, they will find you,"
he said.

"Well, wont' they still be able to watch me
through my identity chip? Surely they'll know I'm not
really dead," I replied.

"Don't worry; I'll take care of it."

"What do you mean when you say you'll 'take
care of it'?" I asked him.

I was growing more sceptical by the moment.
As far as I was concerned, it was only a matter of time
before the state police would come barging into our
housing block, detaining both of us for treason.

Ignoring me, he left the room and slammed
the door behind him. I didn't know what he was

doing, so I decided to remain where I was seated on the couch.

Multiple thoughts coursed through my mind, the first being about my parents. I knew that I was most likely holding onto false hope, but something Rupert had said stuck with me. If he was about to fake my own death, maybe that's what he did for my parents too. Maybe, just maybe, they weren't gone after all.

Rupert came back into the room, this time carrying a larger dull grey metal box. It seemed pretty heavy, as he was carrying it hoisted in both hands slightly above his knees. It didn't help that he was also holding the scrambler, causing him to lose grip from time to time.

"Rupert, can you be honest with me?" I asked him, as he sat back down beside me.

"As long as it doesn't interfere with the mission," he retorted. He was working on opening multiple latches on the metal box.

"Are my..." I hesitated, the words caught in my throat. "Are my parents still alive?"

He stopped fiddling with the box, and turned to face me. "I'm sorry, Megan. Those were really your parents you saw on the news. I know it's hard to take in, and I wish I could give you more time to grieve, but we need to act now before it's too late for you."

"I know that was them in those...those blue body bags. I mean, did you...you know, fake their death too? Are they still alive?"

He brought his hand up to his forehead, wiping sweat along the way. The top of his greying brown hair was matted to his forehead. He placed his hand on my knee, and looked at me staring directly into my eyes.

"I'm sorry. That wasn't part of the plan. Their death wasn't faked by us," he said.

"So, they're really dead?" I took a deep breath in and let it out slowly.

Instead of responding, he returned to fiddling with the latches on the box. By now, he almost had them all removed. Still holding the scrambler tightly in my hands, I watched in silence as he removed the final latch.

As he opened the box, the metal creaked. It was filled with things that I had never seen before, things that were beyond my current comprehension of things. Rupert put his hands in the box, and pulled them out holding a metal sphere.

"This is a grafter," he explained, as he

manipulated the sphere in his hands. "It's used for adding, modifying, and removing identity chips. Right now, I'm going to hack into your chip, and modify it so it can't be read by the housing block. That means that once I do this, you cannot re-enter your unit. Is there anything you need to get from your unit?"

"Well, no. I mean, I had a backpack full of clothes and food. I was planning on running away, but then remembered this," I admitted, pointing to the chip on my left wrist.

"Don't worry; we have plenty of clothes and food at the safe house. Do you need anything else?"

"My vitamins." That was the only thing I could think of. There was nothing that I physically owned that wasn't somehow tied down with a digital link.

"You'll need to stop taking those immediately. We're not sure what's in it, but we figure it can't be good."

"Aren't they supposed to be good for our health? I've never once been sick, and that's because of the vitamin."

"Trust me; there are a bunch of side effects to it. For now, just know that you won't be taking them anymore."

"Okay," I said. "I don't need anything else from home."

With that, he twisted the grafter open and revealed a curved keyboard inside. There were only twelve keys. He pressed three of them, and I felt a small sting on my wrist.

"Okay, it's done," he said. "As of right now, your location is unknown. This won't flag anything in the system until they start looking for you, or curfew; whichever comes first."

"Okay. So, what do we do now?"

"Now, we kill you. We already have a scan of your face. We are going to modify a cadaver to look exactly like you, and then stage your suicide."

"What's a suicide?" I was hearing terms and concepts I had never even heard of before.

Rupert was putting the grafter back together, and placed it back in the metal box. I guess he was ignoring my question.

I still didn't know exactly how all this was going to work. I wasn't really convinced that my identity chip was modified, and I was even less convinced about him faking my death. I assumed he would change the cadaver's identity chip to be identical to mine, but it still didn't seem like a feasible plan to me. The state knew everything.

He was still ignoring me, as he left the room once again. This time, he was gone for a long time. I was about to go and look for him, when he re-emerged.

"Megan, can you come here please?" he asked me.

Obeying, I walked towards him until we were face to face. He led me down a small hallway, until we were standing in front of the wall. He tapped different sequences with his fingers, and then the wall moved.

I followed him into the hidden room, taking everything in. There were sheets of paper everywhere, stacked on the desk, the floor, and the dresser. I had never seen paper in real life before. I learned about its previous use in ancient culture in my History II course, but there was never any indication that it still existed.

I focused my gaze on the rest of the room. There was a small bed in the corner, adjacent to the desk. The walls were light grey and bare.

"What is this place?" I asked.

"It's a temporary safe room. It's by no means

as great as our main one, but it will do until I can move you. You'll have to stay in here, until it's safe for you to leave."

"For how long?"

"Hopefully, no more than a couple of days. It's fully stocked with non-perishable foods. I can't give you anything else until we get to the safe house; there's no electricity coming in or out of the room. As far as the state is concerned, this room does not exist."

"So, I pretty much have to stay here with no say?" There was a hint of exasperation in my voice. I was starting to feel agitated; I had forgotten to take my vitamin today. I was already starting to feel the withdrawal effects. "I need my vitamin."

Raising his hand to his forehead, he sighed. "I'm sorry, Megan. You can no longer take the vitamins. You promised to do as I said. This is not negotiable."

He turned his back to me, as he left the room. I heard the door close, and I was left by myself, alone in the temporary safe room.

Chapter 6

Alone in the temporary safe room, I didn't know what to do. I looked down at my wrist, at my identity chip. It still looked the same; what if it was still active and the state was coming after me?

I didn't know what to think, but I knew I had to think fast. I could either wait here and leave my fate up to Rupert, or I could take off and risk my chances on my own.

Rupert always seemed like a nice guy. I will admit that, on occasion, he acted in peculiar ways, but I was never fazed by it since it never bothered my parents. When he stayed over for dinner one night, he refused to eat anything that was previously freeze-dried, which is almost anything that required heating in the zapper.

I didn't know if I would grow to regret it, but I decided to stay put and take my chances with Rupert. After all, he did say that he promised my parents he'd take care of me.

I was now struggling with my feelings towards the state. I never really thought about my feelings when it came to Grover State. There were no emotions attached. The state made the rules, and we followed them. But why would they make such a rule, as the one for Burdens of the State? How could they justify changing a child's fate so abruptly, due to no fault of their own?

Lying down on the small bed, I pulled the thick dark green cover over myself. I didn't bother getting undressed, and I still kept my shoes on, just in case.

I didn't know what time it was by now. Had they managed to identify my parents yet? Only time would tell if Rupert was indeed telling the truth.

My eyelids became heavy, as I struggled against sleep. I didn't want to lose consciousness, to leave myself vulnerable. My body, however, had a mind of its own. Despite my inner struggle, trying to keep my eyes open, they finally remained closed as I drifted into sleep.

*****

When I woke up, I had no idea what time it was. There wasn't a single piece of technology in this room, and I was too afraid to access my identity chip, even though Rupert said I could no longer be tracked. They could still track all my vitals, and I could still get infractions.

I tried to remember how many things I had to do today, that might lead to me getting an infraction. I already knew that I would be receiving one for missing my education session, but I couldn't think of anything else. As long as I didn't receive five of them, I should be okay.

Swinging my legs over the edge of the bed, I sat up and combed my fingers through my hair. I realized I had to pee, but the washroom was outside of the safe room.

I remembered how Rupert had opened the door, and thought that maybe there was a washroom and the door was just concealed. Scanning the room, I couldn't see any indication of a door. As I was about to give up, my eyes gravitated towards the floor: there was a door leading down below.

Any other time, I would have been deeply puzzled seeing a door leading into the floor. After what I've been through—what I'm still going through—it didn't faze me at all.

Crouching down on my knees, I pulled the handle that protruded from the floor. The door was made of dark grey metal, similar to the box that contained the grafter. The door was heavy, but I managed to open it on my own.

Peering down into the hidden room, I couldn't see anything. The entire room was cast into darkness. I tried to think of a means to produce light, when I realized that I currently had light in this room. How could that be possible, when Rupert had said the room was cut off from electricity?

I raised my head to the ceiling, but failed to see where the light was coming from. There were no light rods hanging from the ceiling, as they did in all housing units.

My eyes scanned the room for a lighting source, when my eyes fell onto a bright ball on the dresser. It didn't seem like it was emitting light; rather, it was bright white.

I scooped the ball up into my hands, and manipulated it around my fingers. The ball was warm to the touch, and very light. I was sure that this was the source of light, as any other source I could think of required electricity. After what I'd been through, I was completely open to the idea that light was emitting from a white ball no bigger than a tennis ball.

Putting my theory to the test, I walked over to the bed and hid the ball under the mattress. All of a sudden, the room was thrown into complete darkness. I retrieved the ball, and light returned to the room. I didn't exactly understand how any of this was possible, but I pushed it to the back of my mind.

Holding onto the ball of light, I dropped my hand into the opening in the floor. The pitch black room was now cast into light. From my position, I could see three desks and six bookshelves. The desks were littered with more paper. The bookshelves were full of actual books. I had never seen a book made of paper before. Our bookshelves were full of literary chips, which were essentially books on a chip. They were read the same way I read my school books.

There was a bunch of other things in the room, which I could not even begin to describe. There were things so far out of the ordinary, that I just couldn't grasp it in my mind. Spotting the ladder leading straight down, I lowered myself into the room while still clutching onto the ball of light.

*****

I couldn't believe that I had just finished reading a whole book that I could physically hold in my hands. It was weird having to look down to read, rather than straight ahead as I usually do. I could touch my fingers to the words; feel the coarseness of the paper in my hands.

After I had looked around the room a few times, I had found it overwhelming. It was too much new information to take in all at once. I had decided to grab a book that was lying open on the desk closest to the ladder, and climbed back up into the safe room.

The book was titled "Aberrations and Extremism in Politics: The Demise of Western Culture" by Dr. Alexandra Reibus. I found it odd that a doctor only had one last name, but maybe that's how it was back then.

This was the first book I've ever read that wasn't authored by the state. All books, regardless of whether it was academic, fiction, or non-fiction, was written and distributed by the state.

The book was written in 2049, but I wasn't entirely sure how long ago that was. Our current year is GY104, pronounced Grover Year one hundred and four. At first I assumed that the author made a mistake, and meant to write GY49, but then she made references to multiple years between 1960 and 2049.

I enjoyed reading the book, even though I barely understood it. It spoke about multiple countries around the world. From the way she described it, it seemed as if a country was the same thing as a state, and the only state in the world today is Grover State.

One thing that did strike me as odd was the mention of Edward Grover. Edward Grover was the founder of Grover State. Before he came along, everyone was hungry, unsheltered, and dying. He created our state, Grover State, and provided every single person with the necessities of life. He was our saviour.

However, there was one inconsistency in the book. Dr. Reibus said that he died in 2038, but that was impossible. Edward Grover, our leader, was still alive today. He was the only person in the entire world who never died.

At first, I thought that it was merely a coincidence. But after seeing him pictured in the book, there was no doubt in my mind that it was the same person. I consciously decided to ignore that, as to not add even more confusion to my current predicament.

There were a lot of mentions of war. We still had wars in Grover State, but they were always outside of the border, and with nature. In the book, she spoke of war where people killed each other. In one chapter, she described a man who went into a crowded mall and exploded a bomb.

I wondered how they had access to weapons. Based on the different violent scenarios she described, from what I could understand, it seemed that citizens were allowed to freely access weapons. I had never held a weapon in my hands, and hoped I never would. If I did, that would mean I would be in the military, and that would be just as bad as being labelled a Burden of the State.

There were a lot of things that I didn't understand. I was certain that the main gist of the book was lost on me, but I was content in the act of reading from the book itself. Maybe Rupert would explain it to me, if he ever came back to get me. I didn't know how much time had passed by, but it felt like forever to me.

Chapter 7

"Megan, wake up," said a voice nearby.

Slowly opening my eyes, I saw Rupert sitting on the foot of the bed. He was holding the scrambler in his left hand and a piece of paper in his right hand.

"Good morning, Rupert," I said as I sat up, leaning my back against the wall.

"It's 6:39 in the evening."

"There's no clock in here, so...yeah."

His eyebrows creased, and he stared at me for a moment before speaking once more.

"Don't speak without holding your scrambler. The geographical locator in your identity chip is disabled, but they're still able to pick up everything else."

I had completely forgotten about the scrambler. He spotted my scrambler on the dresser, and went to get it for me. As he handed it to me, I felt bad that I already messed up.

"I'm sorry, Rupert. I forgot," I said.

"Don't worry about it, Megan. Just be careful in the future. How have you been holding up?"

"Not too bad, I guess." I was about to tell him that I read one of the books from the room below, but I was afraid he might get angry that I didn't ask permission first.

"Great," he said. "We're just about ready to remove your chip, so you won't have to worry about the scrambler for much longer. Samuel is waiting in the living room. Before I ask him to come in, I just wanted to make sure you're okay."

"Yes, I'm fine." I hope I didn't accidentally insult him.

"Are you sure?"

"Yes, I'm sure."

"Okay, then. I'll go get Samuel."

Rupert left the room, and I was left alone once again. I was feeling really guilty about not telling him that I read the book, or that I went down in the hidden room.

Rupert came back into the room, followed by a shorter man with jet black hair. He was wearing a doctor's uniform; he was a high priority citizen. Showing my respect, I knelt down on one knee and saluted him.

"There's no need for that," Samuel said. He extended his arm out to me and helped me to my feet.

"The whole class system is nonsense. We don't abide by any of it."

As he was speaking, I noticed that he wasn't holding a scrambler. My eyes perused his entire body, until my line of sight landed on his left wrist: he had no identity chip. Noticing my gaze, he answered my question without me even having to ask it.

"Yes, my identity chip's been removed. I am no longer part of the system, so to speak. Soon, you won't be either," he said.

"I know it sounds a lot more daunting than it actually is," Rupert interjected, "but I want you to know that we will explain everything to you once you're safe."

Samuel took my left arm and placed it in such a way that it lay raised against his chest. He pressed a button on the sleeve of his uniform, and two robotic hands emerged from his chest and clasped my hand. I had never been in a hospital before, so this was the first time I had an opportunity to see a doctor's uniform up close and personal.

I pressed another button on his sleeve, and this time a tray slid out from his side, and positioned itself directly under his hand. He withdrew two tubes from his pocket, and placed them on the tray.

"This might sting a little, but it will numb your arm so you don't feel any pain," Samuel said.

He opened the tube and applied the blue gel all over my left arm. The gel was cold when it touched my skin, and there was a mild stinging sensation that I've never felt before. I enjoyed the feeling.

He opened the other tube, and then took out a metal cylinder from his pocket.

"Now I'm going to surgically remove your identity chip. I am going to put this chealkra cream on your chip, which will automatically cause it to remove its neurological link with you. You shouldn't feel any pain. Then I'm going to cut it out of your arm." He waved the scalpel to further emphasize his point.

"I'm going to warn you right now, it's not going to look pretty. I will have you patched up, good as new, but the process can be a little hard on the stomach."

As he started placing the chealkra cream on my identity chip, I decided to look away. I had no desire to see the insides of my body, especially while they were being cut into.

To distract myself, I tried to engage Rupert into conversation. Before speaking, I made sure I had the scrambler in hand.

"Rupert, why do you still have your identity chip?" I asked him.

"I'm an infiltrator, unlike Sam here," he replied.

His response confused me. How could Samuel be a doctor, but be called Sam? Only low priority citizens were called by a shortened version of their name.

Samuel started laughing, so I turned to look at him. At that moment, I wish I hadn't: I was face to face with my arm which was conveniently missing a huge chunk. There was so much blood, but I didn't feel any pain.

"I told you it wouldn't be pretty," Samuel said. "Don't be so alarmed at your friend Rupert here, calling me Sam. Shortened names aren't just for those whom you regard as lesser folk."

"I...I...I didn't mean to..." I was taken aback by what he said. I didn't mean to look down on low priority citizens. Everyone had a different value in society, but we were all just people.

"It's okay. No need to start hyperventilating," he reassured me. "I'm not upset at you. I'm upset at the state, for feeding you all these lies, and dehumanizing a whole subset of people, based on their clearly flawed judgment. Boy, I'd like to give them a piece of my mind."

I didn't know how to respond, so I just remained silent. During the rest of the surgical procedure, we all stayed in an eerily calm silence.

*****

I was resting on the bed, my arm bandaged up in gauze. Samuel had used the metal cylinder, a kryg, to repair my skin. A blue laser emitted from the tip, and melted my skin back together. He said that there would be a small scar once it was completely healed, but that it wouldn't really be that noticeable.

Both Rupert and Samuel had left, as soon as they removed my identity chip. They didn't tell me where they were going, but said they would fill me in once they returned.

I was growing uneasy. Regardless of what happened now, I was a traitor to the state. I had removed my identity chip, and that was punishable by death.

I mostly believed what Rupert had told me, but there was still a part of me that doubted him. What if this was a setup? What if he secretly worked for the state, and returned with the state police to arrest me?

All of these conflicting thoughts were doing a number on my sanity. I was feeling more agitated and anxious, ever since I stopped taking my vitamin.

Not able to settle my mind on a single coherent thought, I decided to rest. Hopefully, by the time I awoke, Rupert and Samuel would be back.

*****

When I woke up, my arm was in excruciating pain. I guess the numbing gel wore off. I kept it hung limply against my side, and then got up from bed.

The door to the safe room was closed, but I could hear voices outside. I know that Rupert told me to stay in here until he told me otherwise, but I was becoming claustrophobic. Taking my chances, I opened the door and walked into the living room.

Rupert and Samuel were sitting on the couch, looking at the vision screen on the wall. I was steadily approaching them, fully intent on signalling my presence, when an image on the screen caught my eye.

Prominently displayed on the vision screen was my picture. I stood frozen in place, as I listened to the newscaster give her report.

"...from our Grover State headquarters. We

have received confirmation that the body located in Bay Creek yesterday belonged to Megan Thomas. The state police finalized their investigation, citing her death as accidental.

"It is alleged that the victim, who recently lost both of her parents at this exact location in a horrific car accident, decided to peer into creek. A gust of wind knocked her off balance, which caused her to fall into the creek. As previously reported, the acidity levels in the creek are toxic, and caused her to sustain fatal damage before being able to swim back to shore.

"Barricades will be erected in the coming months, to curtail the rise in accidents—" The image of the newscaster faded away, as the vision screen was abruptly turned off.

"So, that's it then? I'm dead?" I asked no one in particular.

Both men turned around to face me.

"Yes, Megan," Rupert answered. "You're now officially dead."

"How did you do it?"

"I rather not disclose that, at this time. Don't get me wrong, I do trust you. It's just that if our ghosting process was ever compromised, that would be the end of us."

"What's a 'ghosting process'?" They were throwing new things at me, left and center.

"The ghosting process is what you just went through. For all intents and purposes, you are dead. But yet, you are here. You are now a ghost," Rupert explained. "You're in good company. Sam here is a ghost as well."

I really didn't feel like getting more into it, so I accepted his answer. I had so many questions to ask, but now wasn't the time. The only thing I wanted to do now was leave this housing block.

Chapter 8

Last night, Samuel slept over and stayed in the safe room with me. He couldn't stay in the main unit, in case a random unit check was conducted by the police. Once they noticed that the display read 1 occupant, but two people were present, they would start asking questions. That would eventually lead to the discovery that Samuel had no identity chip.

I offered him the bed, but he objected, saying that I was here first. I was really tired, so I didn't argue with him. I laid myself flat on the bed, and propped my left arm over my chest.

Samuel didn't say much before drifting into sleep. I asked about who he used to be, but he didn't really give me much information. He was a high priority citizen, and his assigned life path appeared to be working as a doctor. He didn't tell me anything else.

After he fell asleep, it took me only a few minutes to follow suit.

In the morning, Rupert came in to wake us up. He prepared breakfast for us, which was a welcome change. For the last couple of days, I had been eating the food stocked in the safe room; it wasn't the best selection.

I sat down at the table, and looked at the contents of my plate. I recognized most of the items, but there was a white oval on my plate that wasn't familiar to me. At first, I assumed it was a decoration, but then I saw Samuel take a bite out of his, exposing the yellow interior.

"What is that?" I asked him.

He tried to respond to me with a mouth full of food, but I didn't understand anything he was saying.

"Manners," Rupert said, as he placed a napkin in front of Samuel. He then turned to address me, with a smile on his face. The smile itself was comforting, as I hadn't seen one from him in the last couple of days.

"It's a chicken egg. You're used to eating frozen zapper food, huh? Looks a lot different when it's fresh. If you ask me, it tastes a lot better than a yellow mass of chemicals."

This was the first time I'd ever seen a chicken egg. Now that he explained it, I briefly remembered seeing images of chicken eggs in my Nutrition course. I also remembered that if you ate food directly from an animal, without it being chemically processed by the state, it would lead to disease and death.

"Is it not a bad thing to eat something directly from an animal, without being processed first?" I asked.

"No," Samuel said, having finished eating the food in his mouth. "It's all lies. A bunch of lies from a bunch of liars."

Both Rupert and Samuel continued eating their breakfast. I held the chicken egg in my hand. I hesitated as I brought it to my mouth. I didn't know if it would kill me, but there was only one way to find out. I took a small bite from the egg, and internally rejoiced at how good it tasted.

*****

I was in the safe room alone with Samuel. We were waiting for Rupert to come and get us. He was working his shift at the grocery store, and had to make sure he went so as to not receive an infraction.

Samuel had to stay here with me, because he was technically dead, just like I was. I was starting to get comfortable with this whole situation. The withdrawal symptoms from the vitamins have almost all disappeared, and I was feeling less depressed about my parents' death.

I was excited for Rupert to come and get us. We would finally be going to the safe house tonight. Samuel seemed anxious to get back. Like he said, he doesn't like being in Grover State territory.

I was starting to dislike Grover State. I've never really loved the state, as many did, but I also never really disliked it. It was just a fact, just life. But now that I've been classified as dead, I've never felt freer.

It felt great deciding when I woke up, and no longer doing or not doing things simply to avoid receiving infractions.

I've been spending most of the day going through different books, and taking in a bunch of new information. Before leaving for work, Rupert had shown me the hidden room. He said that I was free to browse through anything I wanted, and apologized for forgetting to show me earlier. I felt guilty that I didn't tell him I had already been in there, so I pretended that it was the first time I saw the room.

Samuel had been quiet for most of the day, and I was growing more bored by the minute. I decided to talk to him. What's the worse he could do? Stay silent?

"Hi, Samuel," I said.

He looked up from the book he was reading, and stared at me. At first he looked angry, but then a smile spread across his face.

"Hey, Megan. I was wondering how long it would take you to strike up a conversation. You got that bored, huh? I guess I'm not that scary after all," he said, with a hint of laughter in his voice.

I was taken aback. I was never afraid of Samuel, and it pained me that he felt as if I was. I did not like it when others thought ill of me.

"I'm not...I mean I wasn't...I didn't mean..." I stammered, not knowing how to express myself.

Samuel laughed, and placed his hand on my shoulder.

"You need to stop being so high strung," he said to me. "Now, I'm not faulting your for it. It's this society, this whole existence. Let me ask you something: Have you ever been outside the borders of Grover State?"

I was about to answer, but he did it for me.

"No, of course not. And why is that?"

This time I didn't say anything, assuming he was going to continue talking. When he didn't say anything, I immediately chimed in, as if channelling my History I textbook.

"Because the only thing outside of our borders is chaos and disaster. We are the only civilization left, and Grove State has been built to ensure our survival. Only members of the military have a chance, albeit a small one, of stepping outside of our borders," I recited.

When I finished speaking, he started clapping his hands slowly, almost as if he were mocking me. When he started chanting "Bravo, bravo," I knew he was making fun of me.

"Spoken like a true product of the state," he said, as he laughed. "I'm just playing around with you. Relax, have some fun. You'll find that things get awfully depressing if you don't invite pleasantness into your life. All joking aside, I would actually like to talk to you. I was waiting until we reached the safe house, but what the hell. Now's as good a time as ever."

"Okay, then. Shoot." It was odd. All of the negative emotions I was feeling a mere minute ago dissipated. It felt comfortable being around him. No one has ever joked around with me, except for my parents on occasion. Joking amongst citizens was generally frowned upon. They usually let it slide if you were a child, but the state police have given infractions on multiple occasions to people who were just joking around. The infractions were classified as a disturbance of the peace.

"All right then. I like this new attitude of yours. How are you holding up with...you know?"

"You mean with my parents' death? It still sucks, and every single day I wake up forgetting that they're gone. I'm coping, I guess. I know that you're not supposed to be sad when someone dies, but I can't help it."

"Let me tell you something that's really important. It's probably the most important thing I'll ever tell you."

And then he stopped talking.

I wasn't sure if I should prod him on, or just let him finish up his thought on his own. I was starting to grow uncomfortable in the silence, but then he starting to speak once again.

"Everything you've been taught your entire life is a lie. The history? Completely false. Grover's nothing but a scam, propagated by a group of narcissistic men, with egos to match those of gods," he said.

"What's a god?" I asked. That was the first

time I ever ran into the term. I couldn't remember ever coming across it in my studies.

"That's right," he said. "I forgot they don't teach you religion in school. A god is basically...you know what, never mind. It will be better for you if you discover on your own. There are a bunch of books in this place. At least half of them reference a god of some sort."

Samuel walked across the room, and picked up a book that he had previously removed from the hidden room. He handed it to me, after flipping over to page 65.

"Here," he said. "Start from this page. It will tell you everything you need to know."

I grabbed the book he handed me, and started reading from page 65:

> *The North Americas have since split from the Greater Republic, and established five colonies. Every one of these colonies, each spearheaded by one of the nefarious men from the Frockle Group, is self-contained within its borders. None of its residents are aware of an outside world, and none of our armies have been able to penetrate their*

borders.

"When was the book written," I asked Samuel.
"A year ago," he replied.

Chapter 9

I spent the rest of the afternoon pouring over the book. Even though I knew what Samuel told me was the truth, I had a hard time wrapping my head around it. The book was titled "Dictatorships in the Modern Era: A Case Study on the North Americas" by S. P. Whitmore and Gregory S. Drias.

When I finally came across references to god, it was a bit much to comprehend. Apparently, religions used to rule the world. From what I gathered, a religion was the belief in a god (or gods, in some cases) that created all life on earth, held by a group of people. It was a hard concept for me to grasps at first. Scientifically speaking, it made no sense whatsoever.

I knew that there were many things that Grover State may have deceived me on, but science could not be faked. At least, I didn't think it could be. As far as I was concerned, the human being derived through natural biological processes, which could be explained by science. At least the book agreed with my current comprehension of science.

I no longer knew what to believe. Almost everything in the book contradicted what I had learned my entire life. Grover State was not a refuge built for our survival and wellbeing; it was a prison.

If I believed everything the book stated, then Grover State was built by a power hungry man, who cut us off from the rest of the world. In addition, we have been lied to this entire time, told that we are the only surviving civilization, when that doesn't appear to be the actual truth.

I decided to relieve myself of immense pressures and headaches, by simply accepting that almost everything that I knew was wrong. I don't know why it was so easy for me to shift my thinking with so little proof, but if I was honest with myself, Grover State never made much sense to me. Yes, I accepted it. However, I did not understand it.

*****

"Sam," I asked, "do you know where exactly this book was written? Are there people beyond the borders of Grover State?"

It felt odd calling Samuel by his shortened name. At the same time, it felt more personal.

"I'm not too sure where it was written. Also, that one year estimate I gave you could be a little off.

The years aren't counted the same, so it's very hard to tell," he replied. "As for beyond our border...your guess is as good as mine. I don't know anyone who has successfully crossed the border and come back. Who knows what happened to them. Maybe the state's right, and it's just nature and dangerous animals.

"A part of me believes that we're not the only ones left, but it's hard to know for sure. What I can tell you for sure is that we've been lied to this entire time. This whole class system...complete malarkey."

I was about to ask him another question, when Rupert came through the door. We hadn't heard the front door open, so we were surprised when we saw him come into the safe room.

He was holding two black robes and two backpacks in his hands. He handed one of each to Samuel and I, and stood in front of us to address us.

"Are you guys ready?" he asked.

I didn't say anything, and Samuel mumbled something that I didn't quite understand. Rupert must have understood it, as a smile spread on his face as he continued talking.

"We have to leave immediately. Put on these cloaks, and do not remove them until you have reached the safe house. I have loaded both of your bags with provisions you will need on your journey.

"You won't have access to any digital maps or databases, so you will have to navigate via this—" He handed Samuel a folded up piece of paper, which seemed to expand to a rather large size. "The cloaks will mask you from all electronic signals, which include all surveillance mechanisms, and state police scans. Just because they can't digitally see you, don't think you're safe. There are still some state police agents who patrol on foot.

"I can't go with you. If I could, I would. The last thing we need is me getting an infraction. I tried to get an exemption, but it didn't pan out. Will you be okay on your own?"

I looked at Samuel, to see what he would say. The only way I'd be okay, was if Samuel would be okay.

"Yes, we should be fine. I'll take care of the kid," Samuel said.

"Once you get to the safe house, tell Chelsea..."

He didn't finish his sentence. Instead, he looked at Samuel, and a knowing look passed from the both of them. I wasn't sure exactly what was going on, but I was too overwhelmed with what Rupert had just said to care.

Samuel started putting on his cloak, so I put mine on as well. It was soft to the touch, and was really comfortable when I put it on. I quickly checked to see if I could identify anything out the ordinary, to explain how it interfered with electronic signals, to render us invisible to the state's digital eyes. The only thing I found was pockets. Nothing on the cloak seemed out of the ordinary.

"Are you ready, Megan?" Rupert asked me.

He sincerely looked as if he cared for my well-being. The only people who have ever cared for me, and expressed it towards me, were my mom and dad. And now they were gone.

"Yes, Rupert. I mean, yes, I wish you were coming along. But I understand. Thanks again for everything," I said.

I wanted to give him a hug, but hesitated. Hugs were only an acceptable form of emotional expression between family members and intimate partners. But then again, didn't I just finish learning that everything the state taught me was a lie.

Against my instincts instilled by the state, I wrapped my arms around Rupert's waist. I felt his hands wrap around my back, and I felt him touch the top of my head.

"Listen to me, Megan. Make sure you do everything Samuel tells you. He's really good at what he does. I should know; I helped train him. I promised your parents I would take care of you, and that's what I plan on doing. When you get to the safe house, hang tight until I get there. Once you get there, you will be safe," he said.

We let go of each other, and I placed my backpack on my back. The bag had multiple straps and compartments; it wasn't like any other bag I had seen before. It felt really heavy on my back.

I looked up at Samuel, and noticed that he had tied most of the straps attached to his bag. I copied him as best as I could, and tied all the buckles on the straps. As soon as I was done, I could feel the difference. My bag didn't seem as heavy now.

"Ready?" Samuel asked me.

I nodded, and followed him as he walked out of the safe room towards the front door.

Rupert grabbed a garbage bag that was sitting near the door, and opened his front door. He walked into the hallway, and turned left towards the garbage chute. The display above the door turned to zero.

Samuel quickly followed behind him, and I followed suit. We turned to the right, and quickened our pace until we got to the staircase.

Fortunately, there wasn't a sensor on the staircase. There was a video surveillance system, but the cloak would hopefully take care of that. Once Samuel checked to ensure that the staircase was empty, we ran down the stairs and through the emergency exit.

Once we stepped in the cool night air, I stopped in my tracks. Right before me, I saw the moon and the stars in the sky. With my own naked eyes, I witnessed myself being enveloped by the darkness.

"Come on, we don't have much time. The state police will be around enforcing the curfew shortly," Samuel whispered.

I snapped myself out of my reverie, and continued following Samuel. He was walking really fast, but not quite running. We stayed close to buildings, and avoided anywhere that had street lights illuminating the path.

After we passed all the housing blocks, Samuel broke into a run. We were in the middle of open space, and we had to clear it as soon as possible.

I changed my walking pace to running, and did my best to catch up to him.

I was starting to get tired. I exercised every day for the mandatory 30 minutes, as did everyone else as part of the Grover State Health Initiative Plan. However, this was different. I was running out of breath, and my lungs were burning.

I saw Samuel run through a park, and lost sight of him behind the trees. To the chagrin of my lungs and legs, I accelerated my pace to get to the park quickly.

As I entered the park and passed the clearing of trees, I looked around for Samuel. He was nowhere to be found.

Chapter 10

I started feeling panicked. I couldn't see Samuel anywhere. I was well past the trees that had previously blocked my field of vision, and was looking in the general direction we were heading.

I didn't know if I should continue running until I found him, or remain where I was. Surely, he would soon realize that I wasn't with him.

I looked around the park. There was no one else around, which was more than expected with the curfew currently in effect. There were no cars passing by, and only a few street lights were visible from here.

I started walking around, unsure of what I should be doing. The more time I spent stationary, the more chances I had of being caught.

I kept on thinking about the worst possible thing that could happen. What if the state police apprehended me? What would happen to me then? I knew that whatever my fate was with them, it would now be far worse than just being classified as a Burden of the State.

I decided to go sit on an empty swing, until

Samuel came back to look for me. The swing was positioned close to the trees, so I could see anyone else approaching before they could see me.

I kicked my feet up into the air, causing the swing to gently sway back and forth. It had been a while since I've been in a park. The last time I was in this particular park, was when my parents brought me here on a Saturday afternoon when I was twelve years old.

I let myself be lulled in by the gentle motion of the swing, kicking my legs to accelerate whenever the speed slowed down. I was trying hard not to panic, and to keep my head clear.

By this time, I was pretty confident that the cloaks were working. Since there were cameras everywhere, the odds were pretty much in their favour if they caught our movement. If we were visible to the state, we surely would have been detained by now.

I continued kicking my feet on the swing, when my eyes caught movement ahead of me. I stopped the swing and firmly planted my feet on the ground, straining to hear what it was.

I couldn't tell if the movement ahead of me was a person, but I felt safe since I was out of their line of sight. I strained my eyes to see if I could decipher the shadow, but nothing became clearer.

The shadow started moving, and I could distinctively make out the outline of a person. I quietly stood up so I was no longer sitting on the swing, and walked towards the trees to further hide myself.

The figure moved closer, and I could make out the state police uniform, and the electro-shield displayed on the back of the uniform.

I started panicking. What if the cloaks didn't work, and the state police knew exactly where I was? What if I was wrong about Rupert and Samuel? What if this whole thing was a cruel joke, for their own amusement?

After all, everything they told me was pretty out there. Did I really believe that the government, that Grover State, has been lying to me from the day I was born? How could there be others out there, without us having ever met them? It just made no sense.

As I saw him walking towards the entrance of the park, I sunk further into the shadows of the trees. Due to everything I've been taught my entire life, I was afraid of nature, even when in parks. Anything could be hiding in those trees.

I hesitated for a brief moment, before forcing myself to walk deeper into the trees. As I made my way past a few trees, I stopped and turned around. I was now hidden from sight, but could still see clearly into the park.

The officer continued walking into the park, and started looking around. He didn't seem like he was looking for anything in particular. It looked like he was just doing one of his normal scans.

After a few minutes, he turned around and walked out of the park. I let out a sigh of relief, and remained hidden in the trees. I was too afraid to leave my hiding spot. It didn't really matter anyways, because from my vantage point I would be able to see Samuel if he came back into the park to look for me.

*****

I was growing restless and scared. I wasn't sure how long I had been waiting in the park because I no longer had my identity chip, but it felt like forever.

I had pretty much convinced myself that I was done for. There was no saving me. I didn't know what would happen to me, come tomorrow morning. At this point, I wished that I had never opened the door when Rupert came knocking. I should have let the state take me, and label me as a Burden of the State.

As I was trying to calm myself down, I felt something touch my shoulder. I jumped up, afraid of what it could be. I quickly turned around, and came face to face with Samuel.

"I thought I lost you, Megan. Stick close by. I'll try to keep a better eye out for you," he said.

I was overcome with joy. All the doubts and fears that had been keeping me company quickly vanished. I swung my arms around him, and squeezed tightly.

"You have no idea how happy I am to see you right now," I said to him, as silently as I could.

After I let go of him, he took his bag off of his back, and rummaged through it. He took out two tubes. They looked like toothpaste tubes, but slightly larger. He uncapped one of them, squeezed out a dark blue gel, and brought it to his mouth.

"What is that?" I asked him.

"Food," he said, as he handed me the other tube.

I uncapped the tube and squeezed it, just as he had done. Unlike his dark blue gel, mine was dark red.

"I know it's not the most appetizing, and I

hate myself for succumbing to this chemical atrocity, but it's what we need if we're going to sustain ourselves until we reach the safe house," he said while eating the gel.

"What is it? Are we eating toothpaste?" There was no discernable taste to the gel; I had no idea what it could be.

"Military grade nutritional sustenance. MGNS, as they so kindly like to refer to it. There's zero percent food in this. It's all chemicals. I'm a fan of science, but this is not food."

Even though he spent the entire time complaining that the gel was just a bunch of chemicals, and could not compare in the least to food, he had no problem finishing up the entire tube.

I had only managed to eat half of my tube. I didn't really feel full, but I also didn't feel hungry. I decided to recap my tube, and I handed it back to Samuel.

He placed it back in his bag, along with his empty tube. He took two round pills from the side pocket, and handed one to me.

"What is it?" I asked.

"Just swallow it," he responded.

I put the pill in my mouth, and was suddenly

surprised to have a mouth full of water. The pill had turned into water, completely filling up my mouth. The water was cool, and felt great as it cascaded down my throat.

Samuel put his bag back onto his back, and we made our way out of the park.

Chapter 11

"How do you feel about sewers?" Samuel asked me.

We had been walking and running for more than three hours now, and I was growing tired. The only thing I knew about sewers was what we were taught in the Education Room. If I remembered correctly, they were transporters of waste.

"Aren't they dirty?" I asked him.

"I guess you'll find out."

We continued walking for a few more minutes. We were now in a part of town that I had never been in before. We were in the housing section of low priority citizens.

As I looked around, there were are a lot of apparent differences. To start with, their housing blocks were a lot smaller than ours. Their lawns were beautifully maintained, as is the standard in the city, but there were no flower beds anywhere.

As we approached the last housing block on the street, Samuel surprised me. Instead of continuing on straight ahead, he turned towards the building and made his way towards the rear emergency exit. I didn't question him; I just followed.

He opened the emergency exit door, and walked down a flight of stairs to where the basement units are located. I followed closely behind, remaining quiet the entire time.

We walked all the way down the hallway, until we were in front of the last unit of the floor. The door display read that there were two occupants inside.

Samuel took out a piece of paper from his pocket, and slid it under the door. We waited in silence for a few seconds, and then the front door slid open.

I followed him inside, and we were greeted by two women. Everyone remained quiet, as the door closed behind us. The two women started walking down their hallway, and we followed behind. We walked past the Education Room, and one of the woman pushed a panel on the wall. A door appeared, and opened into a safe room similar to Rupert's.

In the safe room, both women grabbed scramblers from one of the desks, and turned to face us.

"Sam, I'm glad to see you made it okay!" one of the women exclaimed.

"Of course, Tammy. Would you expect any

less?" he said.

The other woman focused her attention on me, and held me by my shoulders.

"Hi Megan," she said. "Wow, you've grown so much. You probably don't remember me. I'm Amber. I was friends with your parents."

What she said struck me as odd. It was very rare for citizens of different classes to mingle together. The only friends that my parents had—well, the ones that I knew of—were mid priority citizens, just like us.

"How do you know my parents?" I asked her.

Samuel turned around, and looked towards Amber. "Don't mind her, she's still fighting the programmed information in her head. It'll pass over soon." Then he turned to address me. "Don't worry, they don't bite. I promise."

I felt my cheeks turning red, and was embarrassed. I didn't mean to act as if I was better than them. I didn't mean to look down on them because they were low priority citizens.

"Don't worry, Meg," Amber chuckled. I liked the way she said my name, in its shortened version. No one had ever addressed me like that before. Meg.

I sat down at the desk, while all three of them

were engaged in deep conversation. I didn't really hear anything that they said. They weren't explicitly trying to keep their conversation secret from me, but I felt as if they rather I not listen in.

I rummaged through the different items on the desk. Unlike Rupert's desk, theirs was very neatly arranged. There were a bunch of books with papers sticking out of them. Many of the titles were similar to the ones Rupert had.

As I was looking around, I noticed a map of the world on the wall. The world seemed so large, compared to the maps of Grover State I had previously seen. Where Grover State was indicated on our current maps, the United States of America was indicated on theirs.

On their map, Grover State was separated into multiple small factions. I wonder if they were all inhabitable once before? Grover State, as I knew it, was less than a fourth of what one faction represented on this map.

What struck me as odd, more than anything else, was the fact that other states were listed as well. There was a Canada, and a Mexico, and a multitude of others. I had never heard of those states before, or seen them represented on a map. Grover State was supposed to be the extent of the world. A small fraction of it was liveable, and the rest was wild nature.

I was tempted to chalk the map up to a work of fiction, maybe created by Amber or Tammy, but a large part of me doubted it. I knew that this map was most likely the real world map.

I was now used to the fact that almost everything I knew was a lie. When I first learned about all of...this, I thought that I wouldn't be able to process it. I was actually quite surprised with how willingly I accepted what they all told me.

I heard a loud noise, and turned around to see what they were doing. Amber was opening up a door in the floor. It was probably a hidden room, just like Rupert's. I got up from the desk, and went to stand with them.

When I peered inside the opening, all I saw was an empty room staring back at me.

"That's our ticket to the safe house," Samuel said. "It should be nothing but smooth sailing, from here on out."

"I'm sorry we didn't get more time to acquaint ourselves, but we'll be seeing you at the safe house soon," Amber said.

I watched Samuel climb into the empty room, and followed closely behind. I was looking down at my feet while I was descending the ladder, so I didn't really have a chance to check my surroundings until my feet hit solid ground. When I looked up, I noticed a great big hole in the wall, leading into a tunnel.

In my head, I had planned on waving goodbye to Tammy and Amber, but this caught me off guard. How could there be a tunnel in their unit, without the state being aware of it?

"What is...?" I began asking Samuel, but my question slowly tapered off.

Samuel, unaffected by this since he most likely has been here before, walked into the opening of the tunnel. I watched as he reached into his pocket, and retrieved a ball of light, like the one from Rupert's safe room. I didn't know what it was called, so I decided to call it an orb light. He turned around before going further, and beckoned me to follow him.

"This tunnel leads into the sewer system under Grover State. It will bring us about ten kilometres outside of city bounds," he said.

I had started walking towards him, but stops dead in my tracks as he uttered his last sentence. No one ventured outside of city bounds, except for the military. And even they seldom came back from a mission, due to the unforgiving harshness of nature and wild animals roaming free.

"We'll die if we leave the city's borders," I said.

Samuel sighed, and stepped out of the tunnel and back into the empty room. He placed a hand on my shoulder, and steered me towards the tunnel.

"Listen, Megan. Actually, I'm going to start calling you Meg. I like how that sounded when Amber said it," he said.

"Okay," I replied. I wasn't sure how that was supposed to convince me to go into the tunnel, but I was all ears.

He continued, "I promise you that you won't die—well, probably won't die. Can't guarantee anything." He silently chuckled.

"You know, you're not really convincing me here."

"I'm sorry, I'm sorry," he apologized. "In all seriousness, I promise you that you will be safe. The tunnel leads directly under the safe house. There are people there right now, and I assure you they're alive. Or at least, they were before I left." He chuckled again.

"Sam, come on. I'm already freaked out enough here."

Before the last word even came out of my mouth, Samuel had clasped both of his hands together, and a big grin was spreading on his face.

"What?" I asked him.

"You called me 'Sam'," he said. "You're coming along quite fine, if I do say so myself. Which I just did." He chuckled again.

When you take away the immediate threat of danger, Samuel was a pretty fun guy to be around. I started laughing, which was something that I've never really done before. Laughing was also a frowned upon display of emotion.

I've noticed it more and more, that ever since I've stopped taking my daily vitamin, I felt freer and happier. Prior to the last few days, I didn't know that happiness had varying degrees to it.

I smiled at Samuel, and walked towards the tunnel. I heard him walking behind me. Even though I couldn't see his face, I knew that if I turned around I would be greeted with a big smile.

Chapter 12

The tunnel was really warm. Although the cloak wasn't really that thick to begin with, it was causing me to perspire profusely. I thought about asking Samuel if I could take off the cloak for a while, but didn't want to risk him getting mad at me. Everything had been going so well since we entered the tunnel. We haven't yet run into anything that could potentially get in our way.

By now, we had already finished five tubes of MGNS and about two dozen water pills between the both of us. We were well fed and hydrated. The only thing standing in my way was the heat.

The tunnel we had initially entered connected to the sewers, but there was no water in any of them, not even a drop of moisture.

Samuel explained that we were not in fact walking through Grover State sewers, but rather sewers that ran below the state. These sewers were put out of use a long time ago. The state had apparently built a new sewer system, without bothering to reuse the current one, or to block it off from all access.

I was doing my best to keep up with him, but I was finding it harder and harder to do so. I was looking at the back of his bag, as that was the only distinctive thing I could see. I took a few more steps, and looked down to watch my footwork. When I looked back up, I could no longer see Samuel.

I didn't really panic, because the current section we were in was an enclosed tunnel that only went in one direction. Samuel had said it eventually connected back to the sewers, but that shouldn't be for at least another hour or so.

I kept slowing down my pace, trying to ease the pressure on my body. I wasn't doing as well as I previously thought. I think I was becoming dehydrated. I needed water, but Samuel had the water pills. And Samuels was...

"Samuel!" I called out.

I strained to hear any noise in the tunnel, but all I heard was the echo of my voice.

"Samuel!"

I still didn't hear anything. I continued walking forward, hoping to catch up with him. Could he really be so far ahead of me, that he couldn't hear my voice? I knew I was falling behind, but I didn't think I was that far behind.

"Sam?" I meant to shout out his name, but my feeble attempt sounded more like a question.

I still did not hear a single thing, save for the echo of my voice. I kept on moving my feet forward, trying to close the gap between us.

My legs were aching, and my throat was burning. I was so thirsty. If I could just make it a few more minutes, maybe I would finally find Samuel.

I took a few more steps forward, and collapsed on my knees. I knew I needed to get back up, to continue walking, but I didn't know how to convey that to my brain.

I took a deep breath in, and then everything went black.

*****

When I woke up, Samuel was hovering above me. There was a look of concern on his face. It was a look that I was only used to seeing on my mom or dad's face.

"You're awake! Here, open your mouth," I heard Samuel say.

I was blinking my eyes rapidly, as I was trying to regain focus of the tunnel. I could not see what Samuel was doing, but I felt something being forced past my lips, and entering my mouth.

All of a sudden, my mouth was full of water. I swallowed down the water hungrily, and asked him for another water pill.

"What happened?" I asked him.

"Your guess is as good as mine," he replied. "I was going to suggest that we stop for a rest, but I couldn't find you. I walked back down the tunnel, and found you passed out on the floor."

My throat was still burning, but not as much as before.

"It's so hot. Can I take off the cloak?" I asked him. I no longer cared about him being upset. All I cared about was cooling down my body temperature.

I remained lying on the ground, waiting for an answer. When none came, I focused all my energy on getting up. As I looked around for Samuel, I saw him riffling through both of our bags.

"Hey, Samuel, what's going on?" I asked.

I had finally managed to get myself to a seated position. I leaned forward so that all my weight rested on my knees, and used the momentum to propel myself up. That's when I realized why Samuel was being so quiet. My cloak was lying beside him on the floor.

I ran over to him, covering the distance in a few paces. I quickly grabbed the cloak off the ground, and put it back on. As I was arranging it on my body, I heard Samuel speak.

"What happened? I mean...why did you take off the cloak?" he asked.

I couldn't tell if he was angry, or just asking a genuine question. His voice was monotone. It no longer carried the same joy and happiness that it did before we entered the tunnel.

"I'm sorry, I..." I started to apologize, but I didn't know what else to say to him. I didn't even remember taking off the cloak. "I didn't mean to..." My words wavered. There wasn't anything else I could say, the damage had already been done.

We both remained in silence, while he continued rummaging through the bags. I didn't know what he was looking for, nor did I have the slightest idea, but I knew better than to interrupt him to ask.

I continued watching him for a while. The shock of what I had done had put my mind off the dehydration and heat exhaustion. I was starting to feel a bit better, but I still wasn't back to being one hundred percent.

I really wanted to eat a tube of MGNS and swallow a few more water pills, but they were all in the bag he was holding. I was going to wait until he was done, but my mouth acted before receiving directions from my brain.

"Can I have some water and food? I'm hungry and thirsty," I said. My voice was feeble and weak. I was hoping that would make him ease up on me.

Samuel still remained silent. I watched as he rummaged through the bags again. At first I thought he was ignoring me, but then he turned around and handed me two tubes and a handful of water pills.

"Thank you." I eagerly grabbed the two tubes of MGNS and the handful of water pills. I counted the pills as the fell in my hand. He had given me nine of them.

I thought he would at least say something to me, but he returned to rummaging through the bags. At this point, I wasn't entirely sure what he could be looking for. The ground was littered with the contents of both bags, half of which I had no name or context for.

I sat on the floor and leaned my back against the wall. The wall was cool to the touch, the temperature cascading throughout my entire body.

Such a small reaction felt wonderful. I opened up one of the tubes, and squirted out the gel. This one was purple; I haven't tried the purple gel yet. I didn't expect a different taste, as they all pretty much tasted the same.

By the time I finished the entire contents of the tube, squeezing it until every last drop fell into my mouth, I turned around to see what Samuel was up to. He was still rummaging through the bags. This was getting ridiculous, so I decided to get up and walk over to him.

Once I was close enough to touch him, I tapped him on the shoulder. "Come on, Samuel. I get it, I messed up. You don't have to ignore me. I didn't mean to take off the cloak. I don't even remember taking it off. All I remember is that I lost you and I was getting really hot, and then you waking me up a while ago."

He turned around, and it actually seemed as if he was listening to what I was saying. His eyes were softening, and he stopped rummaging through the bags.

"I'm not mad about the cloak. I'm sorry, kid. This isn't about you. I didn't mean to drive you nuts off the wall, being quiet and all," he said.

"You're not mad about the cloaks? But won't they be able to pick us up on the surveillance system? Isn't that why we had to wear them in the first place, so that they can't find us?"

"There's no need to worry. No electronic signal can make its way down here. We're safe. No, you see, the reason why I'm going a little crazy here, is because we've been bugged."

"What do you mean by 'bugged'?" I had no idea what he was referring to.

"I mean this," he said, as he retrieved a small chip from his pocket. I immediately recognized it as a p-chip. A p-chip was a physical tracker that Grover State placed on property they wanted to keep track of. They were usually affixed on items worth a lot of money, like cars.

"I found it in my bag, as I was rummaging to get you another tube of MGNS," he continued. "I don't know if it's active—I would need an identity chip to check that—but I do know that there's no reason for it to be here."

"You think someone put it there? So do you think..." I didn't want to finish my sentence, because I didn't want to face its implications. Regardless, I didn't have to finish my thought, as Samuel knew exactly what I was thinking.

"Don't worry yourself, Megan. I guarantee you, on my life, that it wasn't Rupert. He's like a brother to me. He would never cross me, or the group, like that. He would never do that to you, and soil the memory of your parents."

"What about Amber? Or Tammy? Do you think it was one of them?" I wasn't really sure if I believed one of them had done it, but I couldn't think of anyone else we might have run into.

"No, there's not a chance in hell those two were involved. They've been with the group since day one. They have...let's just say they have ample reasons to want to topple the system. I can't for the life of me figure out who could have bugged us. Rupert packed the bags himself, and he's a very careful guy."

I didn't know what else to say. I wanted to ask him what it meant, that we had been bugged. Did the state police already know that we faked our deaths? Were they lying in wait, ready to catch us once we emerged from the sewers?

Samuel returned to rummaging through the bags. "I think that's the only one," he said, as he started packing the bags back up.

He managed to get everything on the ground back into the bags in record time. I was amazed at how so much could fit into those two little bags. He passed me mine, and slung his on his back.

"You ready, kiddo?" he asked me.

"What about the p-chip?"

"What's done is done. The best thing for us to do now, is to get to the safe house as quickly as possible."

Before continuing on our journey, he dropped the p-chip on the ground and squished it under his foot.

Chapter 13

I wasn't sure how long we had been walking for, but we passed two sewer sections, and were back in another tunnel. I was doing better than before, and was able to keep up with Samuel. I could tell that he had slowed down his pace for me, but he didn't seem to mind.

Even though Samuel had said that electronic signals could not be read from down here in the tunnel, he still kept on his cloak. My temperature had cooled, and I wasn't on the verge of heat exhaustion, so I decided to keep mine on as well. Might as well keep it on, just in case.

I was looking down at my feet, watching their movement as I walked, when we saw a light up ahead. At first I assumed it was a reflection off of Samuel's orb light, but he quickly hid the orb under his cloak, and we were cast into darkness, save for the light at the end of the tunnel.

I felt his hands on my shoulders, and followed him as he pulled me further into the shadows. I could hear him breathing heavily in my ears, as we both watched for movement.

My heart started beating rapidly against my chest, and I was sure he could hear it. I just hoped that whoever else was in here couldn't.

"Don't move," Samuel whispered in my ear.

I felt him move from behind me, and he too disappeared into the shadows. I didn't know what his plan was, so I just remained as still as possible.

I was focusing my attention on the light, but it wasn't moving in any direction, either forward or backwards. As I concentrated, I could tell that the light seemed to be rotating, as if it were searching for something.

I concentrated really hard on keeping the sound of my breath under control. I couldn't disappoint Samuel. I couldn't disappoint Rupert. I had to do my best to remain quiet.

All of a sudden, the light started moving forward, approaching us. At first its speed was rather slow, but then it accelerated as fast as someone running.

I was frozen in place, overtaken by fear. I couldn't move. I couldn't say a thing. I closed my eyes, bracing myself for the impact. I felt myself being thrown on the ground, and my head hit the ground with a thud. I landed right on top of my left arm, and could not have been more thankful that it had healed quickly from the identity chip removal.

I kept my eyes shut, expecting to be addressed by the state police. At least, I would hope we were only facing the wrath of the state police. I think we were now outside of state bounds, and I cringed to think of what creatures lurked in the darkness.

My eyes remained closed, but nothing else happened. No one—or thing—touched me at all. I slowly opened my eyes, and was once again confronted by the darkness.

Realizing that I was alone, I got myself up to a seated position, but still remained on the floor. I was too afraid to move or to make any sudden movement.

"Are you okay?" Samuel whispered in my ear.

The sudden sound of his voice caused me to let out a gasp, and I quickly put my hands over my mouth, hoping that no one else had heard.

"I'm okay. Are you okay? What happened?"

I reached out my hands into the darkness to get a feel for Samuel's location. My hand landed on his shoulder; he was sitting to my right.

I assumed the orb was still hidden in his cloak, since we were in darkness once again. The other light had disappeared, but I still didn't know what it was.

"Try not to be scared. Just hold onto my hand, and follow me. We're going to walk up the tunnel a bit, and go up the ladder."

The calmness of his voice was reassuring, but I was still shaken up about what had just happened. I didn't understand why we needed to leave the tunnel. Didn't he say this was a safe way to get to the safe house?

I didn't say anything, but followed him as he led me by hand. We were walking forward, navigating by dragging our hands against the tunnel's wall. After a few minutes, we stopped moving.

"Climb up the ladder, right behind me. Don't look down or back. Just keep climbing up until you reach an even surface. I'll help pull you up, once I get to the top," Samuel said.

I couldn't see the ladder. I reached out in front of me and felt along the wall, until my hand came to rest on one of the rungs. Even though I couldn't see him climb up the ladder, I could hear him. After giving him what I thought was a reasonable head start, I started climbing behind him.

The ladder was really tall. It felt like I was

climbing for hours, even though it couldn't have been more than a minute. I had never climbed up a ladder this tall before.

When my head poked through the opening, I could see light again. Samuel had placed the orb light on the ground, as he bent down to help pull me up through the opening.

As I started taking in my new surroundings, I realized that we were still in the tunnel, but this seemed to be a hidden part of it. Considering how long it took to climb up the ladder, I thought it was fair to say that this was deliberately built. It was an alcove of sorts.

"What is this place?" I asked Samuel. "Did you build it?"

He was taking off his bag and shoes, and placing them against the base of the tunnel's wall.

"No, no. We found it when we first started using this tunnel access a while ago. We don't know its purpose, but it's safe to bet that no one will be looking for us here. You can't see anything or hear anything from down below. We tend to use this as a...well, I guess you could call it a safe room, of sorts. Sometimes we use it to rest. Sometimes we use it to restock. Right now, we're using it to lay low for a while," he said.

As he was talking, that's when I noticed the various boxes and bags strewn at the far end of the alcove. Some of them were small enough to stuff into my bag. Others seemed too big to be carried by one person alone. As curious as I was about their contents, I was even more curious about what just happened.

Still enclosed in his cloak, Samuel sat down and leaned against the wall. He let out a huge sigh, and extended his feet directly in front of him.

"So," I said, as I stood hovering above him. "What exactly happened down there?"

He looked up at me, and a small grin started to form on the edges of his mouth.

"What happened, is that we just escaped with our lives. That was a close one."

"I figured as much," I replied, as I sat down beside him against the wall.

"Yeah, that was a close one. It's the first time I have ever seen a mobile scanner in person," he said.

"What's a mobile scanner? What does it do?" I didn't know what a mobile scanner was, and tried to recall if I had ever heard the term prior to now.

"It's another one of their surveillance systems.

It's basically a robotic camera that transmits directly to the state police's headquarters. Luckily for us, it can only read electronic signals. Thank goodness we smashed that chip before it came upon us."

"Then why did we have to hide, and keep our voices down?" I was puzzled as to how the mobile scanner could detect us if we didn't have a chip.

"Just a precaution. You never know, you know," he replied.

"Why was it down here?"

"I don't know. I'm as curious about that, as I am about the p-chip I found in my bag. It passed by and didn't detect us. If it had, trust me, we wouldn't be standing—well, sitting—here right now. We're safe," Samuel said.

"Yeah," I added. "For now.

Chapter 14

We had decided it would be best to stay in the alcove in the tunnel, and get some well needed rest. This was the first time that Samuel ever asked my opinion about what we should do, and it felt great to have a say in what we were doing.

Samuel had fallen asleep shortly after we spoke, still leaning against the wall. I tried to nod off as well, but I was having a hard time. Even though he had assured me that we would be safe sleeping here, I still had difficulty feeling safe.

I felt myself falling into a trance, listening to the low hum of Samuel's breathing, with the few snores emanating from his sleeping body.

Leaning against the wall, I started to feel very sleepy. I was having trouble keeping my eyes open, but I struggled against it nonetheless. After a few minutes of fighting myself, I finally gave into the temptation. I laid down on the floor, and closed my eyes. It didn't take long for me to fall into a deep sleep.

*****

I rubbed my eyes as I woke up, and raised myself to a seated position. I was fully expecting to see Samuel up and ready to go, but he was still sleeping against the wall.

I contemplated waking him up, but decided to let him sleep. It would be best for all of us if he was at his strongest once we continued our journey.

Before sleeping, I had placed my bag beside Samuel's. I went to retrieve it, and went back to my spot. Sitting down on the ground, I opened my bag up for the first time.

The first thing I saw when I opened it was two large transparent bottles, each about the size of a can of soda. There was no label on either bottle, but I could tell they were water pills.

Right beside the water pills, there was a large plastic bag filled with tubes of MGNS. I wasn't sure exactly how many were in there, but my best guess without counting was twenty. I went to place the bag beside me, but decided to count them at the last moment. There were thirty-seven tubes in the bag.

The next item I pulled out from the bag was very familiar: It was a scrambler. I wasn't sure why we would need it, considering neither of us had an identity chip, but Rupert must have had a reason to put it in there.

I pulled out another plastic bag that was labelled First Aid Kit. Every unit in Grover State was equipped with a first aid kit, but its contents were not even close to the contents of this bag. This one contained multiple bottles marked as antibiotics, and many other instruments that I had no name for.

In the bottom of the bag, there was a change of clothing. I pulled out the clothes, and noticed that they belonged to me. Rupert must have gone back into my unit and retrieved them from my closet.

There were a few other things in the bag, but I had no idea what they could be. Since Samuel was still fast asleep, I decided to just repack my bag.

As I was placing everything back into my bag, I noticed that there was another pocket that I had yet to explore. I closed the main compartment that I had been looking through, and opened the newly discovered pocket.

Inside of the pocket, there was a book and an envelope. The book didn't have any markings on the outside cover: no title; no author; no nothing. The envelope wasn't addressed to anyone in particular. I was about to place it back into the bag, assuming that it was meant for Samuel, but stopped myself. The book and the envelope were in my bag, the one that Rupert had given me. If he meant for the items to go to Samuel, surely he would have put them in his bag.

I placed the book gently on the ground beside me, and opened the envelope. I hardly ever had an occasion to open envelopes, since almost everything was digital. I enjoyed the sensation of the paper in my hands, as I removed the paper from within it.

My heart accelerated when I read the first line of the letter. It was addressed to me. I fully rested my back against the wall, as I read the beautiful cursive writing, inked in a bold shade of black.

Dear Megan,

I hope that you're doing well on your journey, and that you haven't encountered too many obstacles. I wish that I had the opportunity to adequately train you, but circumstances were thrown our way, which we had no control over.

I want to first and foremost use this letter to assure you that your safety and freedom is my top priority. Your parents were truly two of my closest friends and allies, and I still mourn their death.

As much as I would like to disclose more to you in this letter, I cannot. I would hate to think of what could happen, if sensitive information of our group was obtained by the wrong people.

Once you arrive at the safe house, please seek out Chelsea. She will fill you in on the group, and will hopefully get you started with training.

Please keep your eyes open as you continue your journey, and remain safe. I wish not to bring more undue stress to your journey, but I must leave you with this warning: Be careful around Samuel. He is not to be trusted.

Your friend,
Rupert

All the excitement I had previously felt as I

read the letter evaporated. The last line of Rupert's letter struck me hard. I thought Samuel and Rupert were friends? Why was he telling me not to trust him? Why would he send me off with him, and place my life in his hands, if that's what he truly believed?

I carefully placed the letter back in the envelope, and slipped it into my pocket. I didn't want to leave it lying around, and have Samuel find it.

Right now, I couldn't process what Rupert had told me. I honestly didn't know who to believe anymore. Samuel had been nothing but nice to me, and he even went out of his way to protect me. But, so had Rupert.

To put my mind on other things, I decided to explore the book that he had also given me. There was no indication in the letter as to the importance of the book, so I assumed it was just a present given to alleviate boredom.

As I went to open up the book, I stopped myself. I decided to place the book back into my bag, and keep it for another day. The letter had already agitated me enough. I didn't need to add whatever this book contained to it.

I made sure that my bag looked exactly as it had before, and placed it by my side. Samuel was still asleep, and wasn't showing any signs of waking up soon. Looking at his sleeping form, I tried to imagine him being a threat to me. However much I tried, I just couldn't.

I was still sitting on the floor, and couldn't find any motivation within me to actually get up. A fleeting thought passed my mind: I could leave before he wakes up, and make my escape. But how would I get to the safe house? I had no idea where it was. Even if I knew where it was, I had no idea how to survive on my own.

I was trying to imagine Samuel being cruel to me, being an enemy. I had to admit that he wasn't always the warmest person, but he wasn't mean either.

Looking at him sleep, I decided to stay put and follow Samuel to the safe house. I had no other option, regardless of whether he was a threat or not. He was the only chance I had left for survival.

Chapter 15

"Are you ready to go, kid?" I heard Samuel say, as he jarred me awake.

I guess I must have fallen asleep, but I couldn't remember making a conscious decision to do so. I got up from the floor, and straightened out my cloak.

Samuel already had on his bag, and he seemed revitalized and full of energy. I grabbed my bag from the ground, and slung it on my back.

"Do you need to eat, or anything?" he asked me.

"No, I'm okay. I'll just eat on the way if I get hungry."

Without another word, he lowered himself onto the ladder, and started his descent. I followed closely behind, until we were once again in the main tunnel.

I don't know if it was due to my impromptu nap or to my subconscious mind, but at that time, I completely forgot about the letter Rupert had given me.

The tunnel seemed just as it had before. Samuel was confident that the mobile scanner was long gone, and I trusted him.

I don't know how much longer we had to walk, but I was prepared to give it my all today. I felt well rested, as if I could tackle anything thrown my way.

We spent the next few hours walking in silent. We passed three more sewer sections, and entered a tunnel that branched out into several different directions.

"Where do all of these go?" I asked.

"This one here," he said, pointing to the furthest one to the right, "goes straight to the safe house. As for those other ones, you know, I never really had the chance to find out."

I followed him into the tunnel he had pointed to, and we continued walking until my legs started feeling numb. As I was about to ask him to stop so we could take a break, we emerged into a room.

The room was constructed entirely of brick, and was bare except for the stairs going up to a closed door.

"Welcome to the safe house, Megan," Samuel said, as he patted me on the back.

He led me up the stairs, and knocked on the door. As we waited, I could feel my heart pounding against my chest. I couldn't believe I had actually made it to the safe house.

There was a loud noise on the other side of the door, and then it swung open. We were greeted by a woman and two men. When they saw Samuel, they immediately hugged him.

I was standing awkwardly beside Samuel, hoping that the moment would quickly pass. As soon as they finished hugging him, they acted as if they just noticed me for the first time. Before I knew what was happening, I was quickly enveloped in a huge hug by all three of them.

Everyone was talking at the same time, and I was having difficulties keeping track of what was being said. I didn't really make an effort to understand them; I was too overjoyed at finally reaching my destination.

Everyone eventually walked into the safe house, and I took in my surroundings for the first time. We were in a large room, much like a standard living room in each housing unit. Contrary to those rooms, this living room was large and full of furniture. There were three couches; two in the middle of the room, and one against the wall. There was a wall full of bookshelves, that reached up to the ceiling. I spotted a ladder attached to one of the shelves. There were six desks arranged in random order, each of them equipped with a computer. The computers were larger than the ones I was used to seeing. And none of them had the Grover State logo emblazed on them.

Samuel and one of the men went to go sit down on one of the couches. I watched as they remained deep in conversation, probably catching up on whatever they had been up to.

I was standing, watching Samuel and the man, when I felt a tap on my shoulder.

"Hey. You're Megan, right? I'm Chelsea," the woman introduced herself.

"Hi Chelsea. Yes, that's me. I'm Megan."

"How was your journey?"

As we were talking, she motioned me to one of the couches in the middle of the room. Before answering, I allowed the softness of the couch to envelop me. It seemed like forever since I last felt comfort. This was must more comfortable than a tunnel wall.

"It was okay, I guess," I replied.

As I was thinking of something to ask her, in order to reciprocate and be polite, I realized that she was Chelsea. The same Chelsea that Rupert had referenced in the letter he wrote me. The same Chelsea that Rupert had spoken about with Samuel, back at the safe house. My curiosity got the best of me, and I asked her exactly what was on my mind.

"How do you know Rupert?"

"Oh, how is my wonderful Rupert?" she asked.

"He's okay, I guess. He didn't come with us. He's still in Grover State."

"Rupert is my partner. We've been together ever since... Well, ever since we started this rebellion, I guess. How I miss him. Hopefully, he'll finish up soon and join us."

"Oh, so you're married?"

"Not in the Grover State sense of the word. In our hearts, yes. Anyway, that's enough about Rupert and I. Am I correct to assume that Rupert sent you all the way here with minimal information?"

"You guessed it," I replied. "What are you guys? I'm sorry if I'm being rude. I just have no idea what your group is."

"No need to apologize. We're the Grover State

Rebellion. We work against the government, or at least we're trying to. We started helping people escape when we first found out the truth. Mostly, we just kill people off of the system, remove their identity chips, and move them here. There are many more people who live here, dispersed throughout the house."

"And what exactly is the truth?" I asked.

"The truth is that Grover State is nothing more than a fascist prison run by very horrible people. They've been lying to everyone. There is a world outside of here, and it's a much better place than Grover State."

I let her words sink in. I knew that Grover State wasn't the best place, but I couldn't come up with what would make anywhere else better than here. Was it the food? The people? I couldn't quite grasps onto the concept just yet.

"What do you mean? How is whatever's outside there any better?" I asked her.

As she was getting ready to respond, I took a moment to study her features. Her face was bright. Her long black hair was shiny. She looked happy.

"Have you ever wished you could choose what you do with your life, instead of being told?

Have you ever wanted—well, maybe not yet... Out there, in the real free world, people have children independent of the state. From start to finish, you are part of the process. The procreation. The raising. You're not raising someone else's child. They're a part of you.

"Don't get me wrong. There are an equal amount of people who raise children who are not biologically theirs, and that's just as fulfilling. But the point is this: you get a choice.

"People are also encouraged to show affection, emotion. Imagine! It's actually encouraged to laugh, to play around, to be happy. And all this, for your own personal benefit, and that of those around you. You live your live as you want; not as the government dictates."

After she finished speaking, I waited a few seconds to see if she was going to add anything else. I was hoping she would, because I didn't know how to respond.

"Okay." It was the only thing I could think of to say.

Chelsea laughed, and wrapped her arm around me. "Don't worry. I know it's a lot to take in. I don't expect you to understand everything right off the bat. After all, you've been brainwashed your entire life."

Her laughter was contagious. I felt the corners of my mouth quavers, and then sound erupted: a laugh! I was laughing, and it felt amazing.

Chapter 16

I spent the next few hours sitting on the couch and talking to Chelsea. It was so much fun talking to her. Our conversation bounced between serious, to entertaining, to downright comical.

Laughing was never a big part of my life. It wasn't a big part of any citizen's life, really. The way I felt while laughing was incredible. In my entire life living in Grover State, I've never felt this happy. And, the culprit was just a normal—well, at least to me—conversation.

I found out a lot more about Rupert from Chelsea, than I did from him. Apparently, Rupert was one of the few Grove State Resistance members who actually left the state, and lived to tell about it. I'm not talking about Grover State, the inhabitable part beyond the border. I mean, he left the state and lived to tell about it.

Technically speaking, we were still in Grover State. Beyond the liveable enclosed state border, the rest of the state was unliveable. It was infested by unforgiving nature and savage wildlife.

Rupert actually crossed the border and went into another state. This essentially means, in addition to having to bypass Grover State itself, he had to make his way through all those natural elements.

As she was recounting tales about Rupert, I felt a sharp pang in my stomach. Rupert seemed, just as I had previously thought, like a honest and respectable person. I didn't believe he would try to deceive me. But then, why did he give me that letter saying that I couldn't trust Samuel?

As Chelsea continued talking, I looked around the room. I spotted Samuel, still sitting on the same couch I had seen him on before. The man he was speaking to had since left, and he was now reading a book.

I focused my attention back on Chelsea. I wanted to tell her about the letter that Rupert had given me. Maybe she would be able to help.

I opened my mouth to reveal the contents of the letter to her, but then closed it just as quickly. I couldn't tell her here, not now. Not when Samuel was well within earshot.

She didn't seem to have noticed that I was about to speak, so she continued talking. I was still feeling anxious inside; it had replaced the addicting happiness I had been feeling earlier.

"I just realized, you've been here for a while now, and I haven't offered you anything to eat," Chelsea said. "I'm going to go make myself something to eat. I'll make you some too. You must be hungry."

"Yes," I replied, "I'm starving."

She got up and walked out of the room. I didn't know if I should remain seated, or follow her into the kitchen. I was debating what to do, and then just decided to remain put. I was starting to feel subconscious; it wasn't a feeling I was used to. It slowly dawned on me that I didn't want to do the wrong thing, because I wanted them to like me, to accept me.

I wanted to be part of the Grover State Rebellion. I wanted to help fight, to help take a stand against the state. At the same time, I don't think I really understood what that implied. I knew that my life in Grover State was not free. But, what was freedom? I wasn't quite able to fully comprehend what it was I was missing. Regardless, I still wanted to help.

After a while, Chelsea came back into the living room. She was holding two plates, that appeared to be holding two sandwiches. She sat back down in her seat beside me on the couch, and placed both plates on the coffee table in front of us.

"Don't worry, it's not Grover State food. It's all natural. Real bread. Real meat. Real vegetables. It might taste weird at first, but trust me, it's good for you," she said.

I watched her pick up her sandwich and take a bite from it. The sandwich looked similar to the ones my parents usually purchased from the grocery store, but these ones seemed different. Like the egg Rupert had given me, the food looked as if it could go bad. It's freshness was limited, but I guess that's what made it so good.

Picking up my sandwich, I took a huge bite. The taste was incredible. I'm not sure if I enjoyed it because it tasted that much better than the sandwiches I was used to eating in Grover State, or because I was finally eating something that wasn't coming out of a tube. Regardless, I enjoyed it until the very last bite.

Once we finished eating, I started getting sleepy.

"I'm feeling pretty sleepy. Is there anywhere I can sleep?" I asked her.

"Yes, I think Rupert wanted to give you one of

the bedrooms upstairs. You won't get your own bathroom like the rooms downstairs, but you'll have the room all to yourself. Come on, I'll show you where it is."

I followed her up the staircase, and we walked down a hallway lined with doors. She opened the third door we came across, and led me inside. My first reaction was shock.

Unlike the rooms in our units in Grover State, where all walls were painted the same shade of white, the walls of this room were painted blue. There were images on the wall of people I didn't know, and of items that I've never once encountered.

There was a lamp on the side of the bed that looked odd. The lampshade, rather than the standard grey rounded ones I was used to, was stripped blue and pink.

I focused my attention on the bed, looking at the bedspread; it was white with colourful patterns on it: blue, red, green, and yellow lines.

I looked down at my feet, and noticed for the first time that the floor looked weird, almost like material.

"What kind of floor is that?" I asked.

"It's carpet," she said. "Take off your shoes

and socks, and place your bare feet on it. It's soft."

I complied, and removed my shoes and socks. As soon as my bare feet touched the carpet, my feet were caressed in warmth and softness.

"You must be tired, so I'll let you go to bed. If you need the washroom, it's the first door closest to the staircase. Tomorrow morning, just come down whenever you wake up. Good night," she said.

She waved goodbye, and silently closed the door as she left. I took in my surroundings one last time, and started taking off most of my clothing.

The first item to come off was the cloak. Since I had removed it by accident, I hadn't taken it off until now. It felt great removing it. I carefully folded it and placed it on the chair I spotted in the corner of the room.

The next two items to come off were my shirt and pants. I was finally sleeping somewhere private, and I was looking forward to sleeping unhampered by the feeling of clothing on every inch of my body.

Before getting into bed, I closed the main light, and turned on the lamp. I went under the covers, and drew the comforter up until it was resting snugly under my chin.

I closed my eyes, hoping that sleep would

come quickly. I was tired, and exhausted. My body needed to repair itself. Luckily for me, I fell asleep within the first few minutes of closing my eyes.

Chapter 17

When I woke up the next morning, I put on the same clothes I was wearing the night before, and went downstairs to see if anyone else was awake.

As I descended the staircase, I heard a noise that I wasn't used to hearing. It was the sound of a baby crying. At first I assumed they were watching some type of program on their vision screen. It didn't sound like anything that would play on one of the state provided stations, but they surely must be able to access other stations outside of the state.

At the bottom of the staircase, I saw Chelsea from the back, sitting on one of the couches. I approached her, and went to sit down beside.

"Good morning Chelsea," I said.

As soon as I spoke, I noticed the baby she was holding in her arms, lacking an identity chip. I also noticed that it didn't have a scar on its left arm. If the baby had its identity chip surgically removed, there should be a scar. It would be very faint, but still noticeable.

"Good morning, Megan," Chelsea said. "Meet

Alexis."

She turned the baby so it was now facing me. The crying had subsided, and the baby was now trying to grab at her fingers. I couldn't tell what the gender of the baby was, and the name didn't help.

I had never heard that name before. Maybe she meant to say Alexander or Alexandra. Maybe it was a short form of the baby's name. What I knew for sure, was that Alexis was not on the Grover State list of approved names.

Furthermore, I couldn't quite understand how they would be able to get a child from the state, unless someone who just recently came here was a breeder and had baby, and its death was faked as well. Surely, there was no way the state would let a child disappear like that. They were too valuable.

"Who are its parents?" I asked her.

She cradled Alexis in the crook of her arm, and the baby stopped crying almost immediately. She was looking at the baby as if it was the most prized possession in the world.

"She's mine and Rupert's miracle baby. She was born five months ago. Isn't she beautiful? She's so precious."

Now I was completely stumped. How could

Rupert manage to get a child placed in his home, without having another adult there to raise it. From what Chelsea had told me, she's been here for much more than five months. And how could they fake the death of a child, without it drawing much suspicion? At least I now knew the gender of the baby.

"I don't mean to be rude, but I don't understand how you could have a baby here. Did you guys bring her here, like you brought me? I mean... Actually, I don't know what I mean. I'm confused, really," I admitted.

Chelsea's warm smile never left her face. By now, baby Alexis was fast asleep in her arms, her little hand wrapped around one of Chelsea's fingers.

"Confusion is one of the many things you must deal with when coming to terms with Grover State and the truth. Alexis was not bred, she was born of Rupert and I. We conceived her naturally; you know, the 'old way'," she said.

"But how?" That was the first thing that popped into my head, and my mind failed to filter it before it came out of my mouth. Luckily for me, she didn't seem to take offence.

"I'm not going to lie, it was hard. It took a while, especially after having had those vitamins forced into our bodies from the day we were born. After two years of trying, we conceived Alexis here," she explained.

"But I thought only those chosen by the state to bear children could well, you know, bear them? Was that your life path before you joined the Grover State Rebellion?"

"No. Believe it or not, I was actually a high priority citizen. My full name is Chelsea Hewitt-Despry. My life path was, for the lack of a better word, mind numbing. I was a socialite, and as easy as that may seem, it wasn't. The elite path lacked any meaning.

"Both of my parents were politicians. I think that's what opened my eyes to what Grover State really was, and what it represented. I was never really happy there. Even if I genuinely was, it was frowned upon. Isn't it weird: you're expected to carry on as if you are happy, but it's frowned upon if it truly appears that you are happy. It's so messed up.

"I met Rupert when I first arrived here. I'm not going to lie; it took me a while to warm up to him, due to the class difference. I know it's made-up nonsense, but what can you really do when that's all you've been taught during your entire life?

"It was around that time than Alison and Jason were able to reverse engineer the vitamins manufactured by the state. They weren't able to determine every single ingredient, and they're still working on it to this very day. They have, however, discovered that there's a compound in the vitamin that suppresses all reproductive functions in both women and men. We've been made sterile, so that the state can manufacture our children. That's why those who are chosen to breed are given different vitamins altogether.

"Anyways, fast forward to today, and we have beautiful Alexis here. This is all the proof I need to know that Grover State truly is an evil and horrible place."

I let her words sink in, processing what they meant. If Chelsea and Rupert were able to procreate by themselves, then that meant that we should all be able to. What else did those vitamins do? What other biological functions did they suppress?

"Is that why I'm so happy?" I blurted the question before realizing what I was saying, and immediately felt embarrassed about it.

Chelsea flashed me her warm smile again. She looked down at Alexis, and then back up me.

"Yes Megan, that's one of the many joys that come when you stop taking the vitamin. The vitamins suppress any extreme expression of emotion. That means, no one get depressed, or enraged, or saddened profoundly. If you do get upset, you bounce back pretty quickly. But that also mean things like joy, sheer happiness, and excitement are foreign to us. Our emotions have been suppressed, in order to make the state's rule over us easier. We have been created and moulded to be compliant sheep.

"The vitamins have been out of your system for a while now, no? Most of the side effects should be gone soon, if they're not already."

After she finished speaking, she turned back to admire Alexis sleeping quietly against her chest. I stared at the baby, trying to see if there was anything wrong with it, to warrant the state's manufacturing and distribution of reproductive suppressants. The baby looked normal. As far as I could tell, Alexis was a healthy normal baby.

In every education session I've ever had that broached the topic of reproductive health, I was taught that human reproduction was currently flawed, due to toxins in the environment. That's what the vitamin was for, to make us healthy and repair our immune systems.

It was said that we were no longer able to conceive children naturally, that the human species had lost that inherent population tool. Grover State was put in place to help us recover what we had lost. They claimed that they gave women chosen to breed children special vitamins and intensive biomedical therapy, in order to repair the reproductive damage done to their bodies. That was all a lie.

I looked at Chelsea sitting beside me on the couch. She seemed so happy, so content. Even though I was starting to feel emotions that I had never previously felt, I still couldn't understand how looking at a baby sleeping could make someone feel the happiness portrayed on her face.

I hoped that I would one day be able to experience the full range of emotions that Chelsea displayed. I knew for a fact that I was happier than I used to be, and that there's an unseen feeling I can't describe deep within me, when I feel happy. However, I was nowhere near to being as happy as she was.

Chapter 18

After Chelsea placed Alexis back in her bassinet, she made us breakfast. It was a sandwich like yesterday's meal, but this time there were eggs and bacon inside of it. As I bit into it, the taste activated the pleasure sensors in my brain. Bacon—real bacon—was so delicious.

I still hadn't met anyone else in the safe house. No one else was awake. I also hadn't seen Samuel since I saw him last night. I didn't really feel threatened by him, but I was still bothered by what Rupert had told me in the note.

I patted my pocket, and felt the note there. It was still safely hidden away, exactly where I had placed it. I had desperately wanted to tell Chelsea about the letter last night, but I was now having my doubts. Another thought also crossed my mind, but it was one I was too afraid to explore: what if the note was forged and then planted in my bag, just like the p-chip was planted in Samuel's bag?

Dismissing the thought from my mind, I focused my attention on Chelsea. She started talking a few seconds ago, and I didn't catch anything that she had said prior to now.

"So if you're interested, you're more than welcome to join. I can't promise that it won't be boring, but it will be something different," she said.

I had no idea what she was referring to, but I felt too embarrassed to ask her to repeat herself.

"Sure, okay," I replied.

I was silently hoping that I she would give me more information about what I had agreed to, without me having to prod her for the information.

"That's great. Sarah will be excited. She would love to have company on her foraging. She's been doing it by herself for the past couple of days, because Pierce has been sick with a cold," she said.

Foraging didn't sound too bad. I wasn't entirely sure what the word meant, but I knew I had encountered it somewhere in my past, most likely in one of my education sessions.

I wasn't used to being around people that were sick. If you were sick in Grover State, you went to the hospital and they took care of you. Who would be here to take care of Pierce now that he's sick? Who would be here to take care of me, if I got sick?

"Is he going to be okay?" I asked.

"There's no need for you to worry. It's just a cold, nothing serious. I can tell you're a little spooked. I know you're missing the benefit from the vitamins of not getting sick. But trust me, it's not worth the trade off. Plus, Sarah's a doctor. You don't have anything to worry about."

"Like Samuel?" I asked.

I remembered Samuel when I first saw him. He was the one who operated on me, who surgically removed my identity chip. I had assumed he was a doctor because he was dressed exactly like one.

"No, Samuel's not a doctor. I mean, he is a doctor in the sense that he can do minor procedures and the such. However, he wasn't a doctor during his life in Grover State. At least, I don't think he was because I saw Sarah teach him firsthand most of the things he now knows," she replied.

That caught me off guard. I could have sworn that Samuel had told he was a doctor in his previous life in Grover State, but I could be mistaken. Maybe I was remembering things wrong, and I had merely assumed he was because he looked like the part.

"Don't worry," Chelsea said. "He's really good at it. I can see he did a pretty good job on removing your identity chip."

She pointed to my arm, and I followed her gaze to look at it. She was right, he was a great doctor. The wound was completely healed, and the only reminder of the identity chip was a faint scar.

I was listening to Chelsea recount various tales, most of them involving Rupert and herself, when someone else entered the room.

"Good morning, Chelsea!" she beamed. "You're Megan, right?"

She approached us until she was standing directly in front of me, and extended her hand before me. I shook it.

"That's right, I'm Megan," I said.

I started to internally regret what I had said. I should have said "Good morning" or "It's nice to meet you" instead. I didn't want to come off as being rude. I couldn't lose my only chance at a family.

"It's nice to meet you, Megan," she said.

She was still smiling as she said it. As soon as our hands let go of each other, I realized how ridiculous my thoughts were. I had to stop second guessing myself on everything, and feeling embarrassed about every other word that came out of my mouth. I guessed this was another side effect of not taking the vitamin.

"It's nice to meet you too," I replied.

"Megan said she'll go with you to forage. She can lend an extra hand, since Pierce won't be going back out until he's feeling better," Chelsea said.

"That's great. Are you ready to go, or do you need time to get ready?" Sarah asked me.

"No, I'm ready to go."

I got up from the couch, and waved bye to Chelsea as we made our way out of the living room. I followed Sarah through the kitchen, and into another room that was similar to the living room, but smaller.

Sarah walked straight to the door, and opened it. At first I thought the door led into another room, but when she opened it, I could see outside.

"We're going outside?" I asked. "Isn't that dangerous?"

"Yes, we're going outside. No, it's not dangerous. I promise. Come on," Sarah said.

When I didn't make any indication of moving from my stationary position, she grabbed my hand and slowly led me outside. I was scared, but I didn't resist. However, I did close my eyes.

I continued following Sarah, as she led me by hand. After a few minutes, I realized that we stopped moving, and she had released her hold on my hand.

Holding in my breathe, I carefully opened my eyes.

We were in a field, surrounded by few trees and many small shrubs. Everything was green, but it was a wonderful collage of all its different shades. Other colours popped up here and there: red, blue, black, purple, and even yellow.

Sarah was kneeling in front of a shrub, and picking off the food growing out of it. Well, at least I assumed it was food.

"What's that?" I asked her, pointing at the handful of round red balls in her hand.

"These are berries. We're not sure what they're really called, out there in the real world, but Pierce nicknamed them blood berries, since they're so vividly red," she answered.

I had never seen that type of berry before, not even in any of my education textbooks. I was afraid that they might pose a danger and be poisonous. As I watched her place a few berries in her mouth and chew, I realized that I was worried over nothing. Of course they would be wise enough to test if the berries were poisonous, before feeding them to everyone.

She handed me a basket, and pointed towards a shrub to her left.

"You can pick those berries over there, the yellow ones. Those are sun berries. And yes, they too were named by Pierce," she said, as she let a slight chuckle escape from her lips.

I went to the shrub she indicated, and knelt down in front of it. The berries were bright yellow, and perfectly rounded. I picked off a few at a time, and then dropped my yield into the basket.

After I finished filling up the basket, I got up and returned to where Sarah was. She had finished a while ago, and was fiddling with something in her hands. As soon as she saw me approaching, she quickly hid whatever it was she was holding by quickly placing it in her pocket.

"Hey Megan, are you squeamish?" she asked me.

I didn't understand what she was asking me. I had never previously come across that word.

"Should I be?" I asked.

She laughed, and placed her hand on my back. We started walking away from the field, and into a forest. As we passed more and more trees, and the sunlight became partially blocked due to those mentioned trees, I silently hoped that we weren't walking directly into a wild animal's path.

We walked for a few more minutes until Sarah slowed down her pace. I looked around, and noticed that there were multiple human-made contraptions lying around. Some were on the ground, and others embedded in the trees. Some were made out of metal and plastic, others were made out of wood.

Upon closer inspection, I noticed that many of these contraptions contained something in it. I couldn't make out what they were, but they varied somewhat from box to box, but not by much. I took a step further, and that's when I saw one of them move.

I jumped back, and nearly knocked Sarah down to the ground.

"What in the world is that? It just moved!" I exclaimed.

"Relax, Megan. They're animals. Food. We forage and have traps set up around here so that we always have food close to home. The bigger game—pigs, cows, and the likes—are further from here, and usually require a day's travel to get to. We usually do those expeditions once monthly, and rely on this to supplement whatever we manage to hunt," she said.

I watched as she opened the first trap, and carefully grabbed the animal inside. I immediately recognized it as a rabbit. Although I had never seen one in person, I have seen them illustrated in countless publications.

Holding the rabbit firmly in her arms, she retrieved something from her pocket. As she placed her hand near the rabbit's face, I could make out a white pill. She placed it in front of the rabbit's mouth, and it greedily swallowed it up.

"What did you just give him?" I asked her.

"Deposetic. It's a pill they use out there in the real world. It humanely kills the animal, so that they don't suffer. Just because we need to eat them, it doesn't mean that we should be cruel. It will only take a few minutes for the effects to kick in."

She continued cradling the animal in her arms, much like Chelsea cradled Alexis in hers. After a few more minutes, the animal's eyes slowly closed, and its body stopped moving. She placed the carcass into a black bag she was carrying, careful to place it inside, rather than dropping it in.

I watched Sarah, as she proceeded to do the same thing to all of the animals contained in the other traps. Most of them looked like rabbits, but they were just differently sized and coloured. The last trap seemed to contain a muskrat, but I wasn't entirely sure. I sure wasn't willing to move closer to have a better look.

After she finished collecting all of the trapped animals, she went to each trap to reset them. I waited patiently for her, but didn't offer any help. I wasn't quite ready to be that intimately close with dead animals.

"Okay, we're done here," Sarah said. "We can head back now. The others will be happy to hear we caught a lot of rabbits. Last time, we only caught two and a small fight erupted over who would get them."

"Is rabbit that good?" I asked.

"Personally, I think it's okay. But Pierce, Marshall, and Anne are crazy over it, and I'm sad to say that many ridiculous fights have emerged due to their love of rabbit."

"Wow, I can't wait to try it now," I said. A small chuckle slipped out of my mouth.

We continued walking towards the safe house in silence. The silence wasn't awkward though. Actually, it felt rather comfortable. I took in the sights and surroundings, feeling happy that I had ventured outside beyond the border of Grover State, and still lived to talk about it.

Chapter 19

We were halfway through our journey back to the safe house. I was looking around, taking in all the surroundings I had previously missed, on account of me having my eyes closed the entire time.

We walked through another field of shrubs, and I spotted a small building in the distance that was smaller than a single unit in a housing block. It was built out of metal, and seemed out of place in the green tapestry of nature.

"What's that building over there?" I asked Sarah.

"What building?"

I pointed to the building, and Sarah followed my gaze. I found it odd that she didn't know what I was talking about. Wasn't this the exact same path we had previously taken before? How could she have not seen the building?

Sarah stopped walking, and pulled me by my arm. She flung herself to the ground, and pulled me down with her. We were leaning against a shrub, fully hidden from sight from the building.

"What's going on?" I asked her.

"Shh. Don't talk too loudly. That building wasn't there before. It wasn't there when we left this morning," she said.

"What? Are you being serious? Maybe it's the Grover State Police. Maybe they found us. Maybe they..."

My words trailed off, as my mind became blank. I was frozen in fear. After everything that I had done, after all my efforts, I was going to be arrested by the state police.

"I'm going to go check it out. Stay here," Sarah said.

I didn't argue with her, or offer to go along. I watched as she sprinted from shrub to shrub, closing in on the distance between her and the building. When she was close enough to touch it, she took something out of her pocket. I was too far away to see what it was or what she was doing, but I was confident in her abilities to know that she must have a plan.

She finally stood up to her full height, and pressed her body against the building. She slid her body around the contours of the building until she arrived at the door. After waiting a few minutes, she opened the door and disappeared inside.

I remained in the same position she had left me in, occasionally peering above the shrub to see what she was up to. Now that she had disappeared into the building, my attention was free to focus on the building itself.

The building was made out of metal, and only had a door ruining its smooth aesthetics. As far as I could tell, there weren't any windows or other openings.

Even though she had only disappeared into the building a few minutes ago, I was growing concerned about her safety. I wondered if there was a way I could check up on her, without having to move from my current location. It took me less than a second to snap back to reality and realize that the only way to do so, would be to go up to the building and check.

In my heart, I knew that the correct thing to do was to go into the building to see if Sarah was okay. What if she was hurt? What if there was someone in there, who was hurting her? Even though I knew this, I still found myself frozen in place.

It's okay, you can this, I thought to myself. All I had to do was get up. Just get up, one step at a time.

If something had happened to her, surely there was no chance for me.

Mustering up all the courage I could find within myself, I stood up from behind the shrub. I didn't bother crouching and darting from shrub to shrub as she had. If there was someone in the building, or if someone was watching us from somewhere, they knew where we were.

I slowly walked up to the front door, forcing courage into every step that I took. When I came face to face with the door, I stopped in my tracks, confused. There was no door knob or handle on the door. There was no slot or other way to indicate that the door could be opened. I slowly ran my hand across the door to feel for a hidden opening, when it slid open by itself.

I waited until the door was fully open before steeping closer to peer into the building. All I saw was a empty room with two similar doors facing each other from different directions.

I walk to the door closest to my right, and touched it. Just like the front door had, the door slid open. This time, I didn't wait until it was fully open. As soon as there was enough room to squeeze my body through, I walked into the room.

This room was full of electronics. The only technologies I recognized were the computers spread on top of six different desks, and the vision screen that took up the entire wall facing the door. Everything appeared to be turned off. Although I couldn't name the majority of the item in that room, I knew without a doubt that it all belonged to Grover State.

The room wasn't that large, so I could quickly tell that Sarah wasn't in here. She must be in the other room. Before leaving the room, a small metal box caught my eye. There were no markings on it, and it felt incredibly heavy for its size as I picked it up. Carrying the mysterious box in hand, I left the room.

As soon as the door to the other room opened, I immediately saw Sarah. She was sitting with her legs crossed on the floor, looking through what appeared to be a book.

"Hey Sarah, found anything interesting?" I asked as I approached her.

"It looks like Grover State doesn't trust all of its information to its computers. Look at this," she said, as she repositioned the book to face me.

As I peered down at the what she was showing

me, my heart sank. Written in bright black bold ink was my name, along with my parents, Sarah's, Rupert's, Chelsea's, every other member of the Grover State Rebellion. The only name missing was Alexis.

"What is that? Why are our names written down?" I asked her, my voice barely above a whisper.

"I have no idea," she replied. "Don't worry about keeping your voice down. There's no one else here, and there aren't any electronic signals transmitting to or from the building. For the life of me, I can't figure out how this appeared in the few hours that we were gone. What's that?" She pointed at the box I was holding in my hands.

"Not sure. It was in the other room. I just grabbed it. Anyways, could it maybe be from out there? You know, from somewhere outside of Grover State?" I hopefully asked.

"I'm sorry to squash your hopes, but no. This is definitely from Grover State. It looks like one of the portable bases the military has, but it's smaller than the ones I've seen before."

"You've seen a military base before? I thought you were a doctor? I mean, that's what Chelsea told me."

"I was. Still am. I've never seen a military base until I joined the rebellion. Chloe and I infiltrated a base a while back on a fact-finding mission. It was similar to this one, but much larger."

As I learned that we were standing in a military base, I looked around and noticed many clues that I had previously overlooked when coming into the room. There was a huge cabinet that took up most of the left wall, full of tubes of MGNS. Another wall was mounted full of weaponry. I had never seen a weapon in person until just now.

"Do you think they're after us? I mean, yes, clearly they're after us. But I mean, do you think they know where we are?" I asked her.

Sarah got up from the floor, closing the book and tucking it under her arm.

"I don't know for sure, but I'm going to go the safe route and assume yes. We have to get back to the safe house and warn the others. Here, fill this up with those MGNS tubes," she said, as she threw a black bag at me.

I quickly went over to the cabinet and filled the bag up with MGNS tubes. When the bag was brimming to the top with tubes, I turned around to see what Sarah was up to. She had a similar bag strapped on her back. I wasn't sure what was in it, but I could tell it was full.

"Grab a few of the weapons. Just grab anything, it doesn't matter. As much as you can carry," she directed me.

Facing the wall, I stared at the weapons available for my choosing. I decided to grab the guns, because the other weapons seemed like they were meant for close range combat. That wasn't a combat arrangement that I liked.

I followed Sarah out of the building, and the door closed silently behind us. She was carrying a lot of equipment, but it didn't appear to be weighing her down. In addition to the bag I had seen before, she had two other bags that I assumed were filled with weaponry. She was carrying six guns and a long stick, that I assumed was weapon as well. I was carrying seven guns, varying from pocket-sized, to half my height.

"Oh, we forgot the bag of rabbits and the berries!" I exclaimed, as I realized all our food we had gathered had been left behind in the building.

"Doesn't matter," Sarah said. "We won't have any time to cook any of the rabbits. There are berries everywhere; we'll make due. We need to leave as soon as we get to the safe house."

"Yes, I guess you're right."

We walked in silence towards the safe house. This time, the silence wasn't comfortable. The silence was filled with taunts of danger. The only thought running through my head was that I had lost everything, before it was even mine.

Chapter 20

I woke up to Sarah sitting beside me. My head was hurting; it felt as if someone had punched me directly in the side of my skull. I brought my hand up and felt around my head. Luckily, there was no blood.

I was lying outside on the floor, in the forest. It could very well have been the one we had caught the rabbits in, but I really couldn't tell. All trees pretty much looked the same to me. I hadn't been out in nature long enough to distinguish anything.

"You're awake! Megan, are you okay?" Sarah asked me.

As soon as she saw that I had regained consciousness, she jumped up and sat close enough to me that our thighs touched.

"What happened?" I asked her.

"We were attacked, as we were approaching the safe house. There were three Grover State Military soldiers lying in wait for us. We would have been dead—or worse, captured—were it not for Sam. He managed to pick two of them off with his gun, and I finished the other one off with this." She reached into the waistband of her pants and pulled out a small revolver.

I tried to process everything as quickly as I could. Grover State had found us, and we were now actively being pursued. I didn't have much, but I had my life. I knew I did not want to die, and I was willing to do anything to ensure my survival.

"What do we do?" I asked her.

"For now, just rest. We'll sit and wait for Sam. He went back to the safe house to pick up a few supplies, and to see if he can find anyone else."

I looked deep into Sarah's eyes, and there was no happiness there. However, there was no despair there either. What I saw reflected in her was will and determination, and I tried to emulate that.

"Are we safe here?" I asked.

"We should be. As soon as we finished them off, we ran as fast as we could into the forest. I scanned it, and there are no electronic signals nearby. It's not a guarantee that there aren't any more soldiers lying in wait, but it seems as secure as we can hope for right now."

As bad as this situation was, I was relieved that I wasn't alone. Sarah was here by my side, and soon everyone else would be too. If I was on my own,

I would have been dead a long time ago. But maybe if I had not of arrived here in the first place, this never would have happened.

My voice quavered and my heart beat accelerated, but I forced myself to address her.

"Sarah, be honest with me. Did they find us because of me? Is it my fault?" I asked.

"You know what Megan," she said, "I'm going to be honest with you, because I don't think anyone else has. Don't get me wrong, they haven't kept you in the dark out of malice. I think they're trying to protect and baby you, but there's no time for that anymore.

"Do I think it's your fault? No, I don't. And even if it was, it doesn't matter. You're one of us, whether you like it or not. I could have easily escaped those soldiers if Sam hadn't of shown up, but I wouldn't have. Do you know why? Because they would have killed you. I would never leave another to that fate, especially a member of the rebellion.

"I know we don't know each other very well, but I knew your parents. We all knew your parents, and they knew us. We're a family. Good and bad, it's all there. The only way to fight for our freedom, is to fight together."

When she finished speaking, I nodded my head to show that I had heard what she said.

"Thanks," I said.

"I wasn't saying it to be nice; it's the truth. Anyways, they would of found us eventually. I was just hoping we would have had time to execute the plan before everything got shot to hell."

Since meeting Rupert, everyone had been eluding to a plan or mission, but they never mentioned any details. I was tired of being kept in the dark, and treated like a child.

"What's the plan?" I asked point blank.

"No one ever told you?"

"No."

"To put it bluntly, we were going to destroy the government, from the inside out. That's pretty much it," she said.

Her reply still didn't answer my question. I felt as if she was deliberately keeping information from me, by being vague with her answer. Of course they wanted to destroy Grover State. As I understood it, that was the whole points of the Grover State Rebellion.

I let her reply stew in my head. I had so many more questions to ask, but I didn't trust she would give me complete answers. I tried not to judge her too harshly. She had, after all, saved my life. The least I could do was give her the benefit of the doubt. I was assuming that her reply was a refusal to reveal further information, but there was only one way to find out.

"Please don't take this the wrong way, but your answer didn't really answer my question. I know that you guys want to destroy Grover State. That's pretty much the point of this group, no? Do you not trust me?" I asked.

As soon as the last word left my lips, I saw Sarah's demeanour change. He face was contorted, and she looked pained. My first instinct was to feel bad about what I had just said. I should have just kept my mouth shut. But a voice within me urged me to stick to my guns, and I kept eye contact with her.

She stared at me for a few minutes, but I didn't back down. The only way to keep myself safe was to know what I was up against. I no longer wanted to blindly follow as people just told me what to do. Finally, she spoke.

"Our plan was to infiltrate the government. Once we achieved that, we would have been able to destroy it from the inside. You know Edward Grover, the leader and founder of Grover State? You must have noticed that it's been the same guy in power forever. Nothing ever changes. Same face. Same look. No difference.

"A while back, we discovered that the real Edward Grover died shortly after creating Grover State. Since then, leaders have had their faces surgically modified in order to look exactly like him. They're all replicas. Want to know the reason why they never seem to age? They go under the knife once a year to remove any signs of aging, and make Grover appear unchanged.

"Once we found that out, we came up with a plan. Actually, your parents are the ones who originally came up with it. The plan was to break into the government building, find Edward Grover, and kill him. Your father was going to undergo the same procedure to change his face into Edward's and he was going to pretend to be him. Once achieved, we were going to work from the inside to destroy them.

"It doesn't really matter anymore, because your parents are dead now. I mean, maybe Rupert or Sam could do it, but something tells me they wouldn't be willing to live the rest of their lives in Edward Grover's face.

"I guess you could say that right now, we're pretty much flying by the seat of our pants without a plan. Maybe Rupert has thought of something else while he's holed up in Grover State, but I'm not holding my breath. That's pretty much it."

When she brought up my parents' death, it pulled at my heart strings. I didn't like how she had said my "parents are dead now". It was very insensitive. She spoke of them as if she were speaking of a lost book.

I didn't say anything to her in response, and she didn't say anything else either. I don't know exactly where my feelings were originating from, but I was feeling very upset and irritable.

"Megan, are you okay?" Sarah asked me.

By now I had turned my back to her, and was facing a tree. I ignored her, and continued staring blankly at the tree. I heard the leaves rustling under her weight as she got up and walked towards me.

"Megan?"

I remained silent.

"Megan, you can't just ignore me. I don't know where your attitude is coming from, but you've got to smarten up. Do you understand that we are in a life and death situation? We were literally this close from being killed or captured by those soldiers," Sarah said to me.

I couldn't contain it anymore. A rush of emotions took over my mental faculties, and I just lost it.

"I don't care, Sarah! Just shut up!" I yelled at her.

She was taken aback by my sudden outburst, and recoiled a little. She quickly recomposed her, and tried to place a hand on my shoulder. As soon as she touched me, I hit her hand away.

"Don't touch me! Just leave me alone!" I continued yelling.

I was feeling all this rage inside, but I didn't know why. Why was I so angry with Sarah? She was a nice person, and had been very friendly towards me.

As suddenly as the rage had hit me, it was now replaced by feelings of sadness and despair. As the first tear I had ever shed slid down my face, I realized why I was upset.

"They're gone. They're just gone. I didn't get a chance to say goodbye. I loved them. I still love them. Why do I miss them so much?" I sobbed.

I felt Sarah wrap her arms around me in an embrace. I continued crying with my head buried in her shoulder. She gently navigated us towards the ground, until we were sitting with our backs against the tree I had been staring at.

"I don't understand," I continued. "I didn't feel like this when they died. Not even when I saw their bodies on the vision screen. Why do I feel like this now?"

She ran her hand through a few strands of hair that had fallen over my eyes, and tucked them behind my ear.

"Because you're feeling. You're experiencing emotions, the way they were meant to be felt. You no longer have the vitamin circulating in your system. There's nothing left to suppress you being you," she said.

"But it hurts so much. It was better the way it was before I stopped taking the vitamin. I want a vitamin. I need a vitamin."

"No, you don't. It may seem easier to not feel, but it's not better. I know it feels like the end of the world, but it's not. You're not alone," Sarah said.

I burst into another fit, and this time tears were streaming down my face. Sarah pulled me in closer to her, so that she was now holding me with her arms wrapped around my back. We stayed in that position until, exhausted from crying, I fell asleep.

Chapter 21

I woke up to Sarah shaking me awake. I groggily obliged, and forced my eyes open.

"I'm sorry I had to wake you up so abruptly, but Sam just got back from the safe house," she said.

Upon hearing those words, I immediately picked myself up off the ground. I felt better than I had prior to falling asleep. I think all the crying I did allowed me to clear my head, and be focused once more. I held on to the memory for a few seconds, before putting it aside to focus on what was going on in the present.

"Where do we go now?" I asked her.

"I'm not too sure. I guess it depends on what Sam tells us. He wanted to wait until you woke up, before telling us what he found at the safe house."

Upon hearing those words, my cheeks flushed and a sense of importance coursed through me. Never would I have thought that they would have waited for me before talking about important information. For the first time, I truly felt like I was part of the group, rather than a burden just tagging along and making their journey more difficult.

I looked around for Samuel, but I couldn't see him. As I was scanning the area, I noticed Chelsea was sitting against a tree, cradling Alexis. I walked over to her, happy to see that she was fine.

"Hi Chelsea. How are you?" I asked, as I sat down beside her.

Alexis was fast asleep in her arms, with her chin angled upwards towards her mother. She looked peaceful and serene, quite a contrast to what we were experiencing.

"Hi Megan. I'm glad to see you're okay. When I heard that you and Sarah had been attacked, I feared for the worst," she said.

"Was the safe house attacked?" I was curious to know. I couldn't wait until Samuel told us.

"In all honesty, I don't know. I was sitting on the couch feeding Alexis, when Sam ran into the room and told me I had to leave immediately. He gave me a bag full of supplies, and told me to wait for him down in the basement, where the tunnel entrance is. I couldn't really hear anything down there, so I don't know what happened. He still hasn't told me anything. I'm as behind on information as you are," she said.

She didn't seem as happy and upbeat as when I last saw her, but that was more than understandable under the circumstances. Although she could be happier, there was still a hint of hope and joy in her eyes. I had a suspicion that it was mostly for Alexis, because she seemed to struggle through it.

She forced a smile on her face as she looked at Alexis, and then back at me. I felt bad, not knowing how to comfort her. I didn't know if I should do anything, or whether or not she was expecting me to do something.

We remained in silence until we both heard Samuel approaching. Sarah was walking close to him, talking away as he slowly nodded in response. When they got close enough for us to hear, Sarah stopped talking.

When Samuel saw me, he bent down and grabbed me in a hug and squeezed tightly. It was unexpected, but welcome at the same time. It felt great to have people care that much about me.

"I'm so glad you're safe, kid. Rupert would have had my head off, if anything happened to you. Are you okay? Did you get hurt?" he asked.

"Just my head, but it's okay," I replied.

Letting go of me, he stood back up and placed himself so he was facing all three of us.

"We were attacked yesterday by soldiers from the Grover State military. All the soldiers that attacked us have been taken care of, but there could be more on the way," he explained.

"I don't know exactly where they came from, but they completely caught us off guard. Pierce was the one who alerted me to them. As soon as he told me, I immediately went to find Chelsea and got her to hide underground near the tunnel. Someone needed to protect Alexis. We couldn't all fight and keep her safe, so I had to take Chelsea out of the game. Before I continue, please understand that Chelsea did not ask to be benched out of the fight; I told her to stay out of it, for the sake of Alexis.

"I had to think quickly on my feet, and I chose to go outside to help Sarah and Megan. While I was outside, I guess more soldiers entered the house—"

"Where's Pierce?" Sarah interrupted to asked him.

At hearing her question, Samuel put his head down to his chest, and heaved out a huge sigh.

"I was getting there," he said. "After Sarah and I fought the soldiers near the safe house, we realized Megan had been knocked unconscious. At first we thought that... Well, that's not important anymore. The important thing was that she was still alive, so I picked her up and carried her, and followed Sarah until we enmeshed ourselves deep within the forest. I checked the perimeter to make sure it was safe, and then I headed back to the safe house to help everybody else out, and move them here.

"Once I arrived at the safe house, I immediately went down into the tunnel and retrieved Chelsea and Alexis. She didn't know what was going on. This is the first time she's hearing an account, along with you two. Thankfully, the soldiers hadn't discovered how to access the tunnel from the safe house.

"I'm sorry that I can't soften this news, but we have to face facts. I did my best to save everyone, but I wasn't able to."

We waited for Samuel to finish recounting the events that had happened, but he didn't say anything else. All three of us looked at each other, as we realized what his last words implied.

"Pierce is gone? He's dead?" Sarah asked.

When Samuel didn't answer her, she stood in front of him and grabbed his arms. She lightly shook him, trying to get him to snap out of whatever state he was in.

"Dammit Sam, answer me," she bellowed at him.

"Yes. I mean no," Samuel finally said. "I checked the entire house, top to bottom. I couldn't find anyone else. They were all gone. No bodies though. I think the soldiers took them to..." His words trailed off, but Sarah picked up right where he left off.

"They arrested them," she said in a monotone voice. "As we stand here, speaking about them, they're probably being submitted to re-education in one of those camps. There's no telling what hell they're going through right now."

After that, no one said anything for a while. Sarah and Samuel had both joined us on the ground, and were leaning against a tree adjacent to ours. No one looked at anyone else. It felt as if everyone just gave up. Mustering up all the courage I could find within myself, I spoke up.

"We have to go back to Grover State and save them," I stated. There was a slight hint of a quiver in my voice, but otherwise I was standing strongly behind my words.

Chelsea was the first one to look at me and to respond.

"We can't," she said. "We lost almost everyone at the safe house. Pierce, Adam, George, Regina, Malcolm, Ashley, Sandra, Cindy, Daryl, Marilyn, Chloe, Marshall, Anne: they're all gone. Add that to Amanda and Lucas, the key players of our plan, and the Grover State Rebellion is no more."

"She's right, kid," Samuel interjected. "The Grover State Rebellion is dead."

"No, it's not," I said. "We're still here, alive and well. Yes, we might have taken a beating, and they managed to capture most of our group, but you're missing the point. We're still here. Standing at the ready, able to fight and take back what was stolen from us."

"That's a really nifty little speech you've got there, kid, but you don't understand the enormity of what this means. Grover State knows about the Grover State Rebellion. They found our safe house, and captured most of our people. What's to say that we wouldn't be walking into a trap, if we go back into that retched place?" Sam said.

They were resisting against what I was saying, but I didn't give up. I persevered, and continued my impromptu speech.

"Then I guess we go and find out," I continued. "I'm sorry, but I didn't go through all of this to end up living in the forest, of all places. I would have been better off labelled as a Burden of the State, if this is all I have to look forward to. We have to go back, we have to save them."

Everyone remained quiet, but now they were all looking at me. Three pairs of eyes were focused on mine, digesting what I had just said. Sarah was the first one to pipe up.

"I agree with Megan. The Grover State Rebellion is not dead. I'm looking around, and I see four strong and able members. We still have some infiltrators hiding out in the state. She's right. The game isn't over just yet. We might be facing a minor setback, but could you live with yourselves if we didn't do anything to help those of us that were captured. If Pierce were standing here in any one of our place, I guarantee you he'd spearhead a one man attack if he had to, to come and rescue us. We owe it to them. They're our family," she said.

I could see that Chelsea and Samuel were slowly coming around. Sarah looked at me, and flashed me a beaming smile. I was overcome with glee and joy, despite the serious predicament we were facing.

"You're right, Meg," Samuel said.

"What are we waiting for," Chelsea said. "Let's go."

Without another word being said between either of us, we silently gathered all of our things and headed out of the forest.

Chapter 22

We were walking towards the safe house, on a mission to save our fellow Grover State Rebellion members. On a few occasions, Samuel went ahead of the group to make sure that there weren't any Grover State soldiers lying in wait or any other traps set.

Samuel was walking ahead of the pack, followed by me, Chelsea and Alexis, with Sarah holding up the rear. We managed to walk all the way back to the safe house without any incident.

When we arrived at the safe house, Samuel went in ahead of us to make sure there was no one else around. Once he finished his sweep, we all went down into the basement where the tunnel was located, and proceeded on our journey.

The journey wasn't as scary as when I first took it. This time, I mostly knew what I was facing and what to expect. Before we passed through the first sewer junction, Sarah took out a device from her pocket—the same one she had taken out when we found the military base—and scanned the tunnel for electronic signals. Once it was confirmed that there weren't any, we continued walking forward.

The only stop we made during our journey was at the alcove. In the fight between the Grover State soldiers and us, we had managed to lose all of the weapons we had retrieved from the military base. The only items that survived were the book Sarah had taken, and the box I had found.

Samuel opened up a few of the boxes, and grabbed four of the bags. He stuffed them with as many weapons as he possibly could, and re-closed the lids on the boxes. He gave Sarah and I each a bag to hold, and he held onto two himself. He didn't give any to Chelsea, because she was holding onto Alexis and already had a large bag strapped to her back.

Even though we were beyond tired, we didn't stop to rest. My legs were burning, and my body was becoming overheated again. I really needed to stop and take a break, but I didn't want to be the one that made the group stop.

Luckily, after a few more steps, Chelsea stopped and called out to the group.

"I think we should rest here. It seems pretty safe. We can take turns being on watch. I need to feed Alexis, and we need to rest," Chelsea said.

"I guess this is as good enough a place as any.

You girls get yourselves as comfortable as possible and get some rest. I'll take the first watch," Samuel said.

"I'll take the second," Sarah said. "Make sure you wake me up first, and let those two sleep."

I nodded my head in agreement, and began settling myself on the floor. It only took a few minutes before I ended up falling asleep.

*****

"Wake up Megan, it's your turn to stand watch," Sarah said, as she gently woke me up.

Brushing the sleep away from my eyes, I raised my body until I was sitting in a mostly vertical position.

"Okay," I said. "Enjoy your rest."

"If you get tired, wake up Chelsea. It's her turn to stand watch next. If she's too tired, just wake up Sam or myself. If you don't mind taking over the watch for a bit, I just need a little shut eye," she said.

"Okay," I repeated.

Without another word, I watched as she laid her body erect on the floor, and fell asleep within a matter of mere seconds.

I was still tired, but I had enough energy in me to stand watch for a while. When we had first gone to sleep, Samuel had turned off the orb light. We were cast in darkness, and I couldn't see much further than the outlines of their sleeping bodies.

I looked at Chelsea sleeping with Alexis. She wasn't fully lying on the ground. She had placed her body in such as way that it was partially supported by the wall, and Alexis was lying in her opposing arm. I guessed that she placed herself that way so there was no risk of crushing baby Alexis while she was sleeping.

Samuel was sleeping with his back turned to me. I could see the gently rise and descent of his chest as he breathed in and out; his shoulders would raise up into the air as he took in a breath, and then would sink back down towards the ground as he let it out.

Sarah was fast asleep by the time I focused my attention back on her. I was pretty sure that I would have a lot of difficulty waking her up, if I needed to at the moment.

Leaning back against the wall, I tried to keep my mind focused on something, on anything. I could feel sleep fighting against me, urging me to close my eyes, just for a moment. I knew that if I gave in, I would soon fall asleep and leave the group

177

defenceless. I couldn't do that to them.

I caught myself nodding off a few times, but quickly jerked my head back up, reawakening my sense. On the fourth time it happened, I decided to stand up and stretch my legs. I knew that there wouldn't be a fourth time, because I wouldn't wake up the next time I nodded off.

I kicked out my legs and stretched out my arms. There wasn't anything at all to do, and I was quickly growing bored. I realized that I had been finding it harder and harder to be content when my time was filled with emptiness. I guess that was another side effect of no longer taking the vitamin.

I sat back down on the ground, and brought my knees up to my chest. Cradling my hands around my legs, I rested my head in the crook of my knees.

"I can take over for you, if you want," I heard a voice say above me.

I jumped up at the sound, and found myself looking up at Chelsea. I noticed that she wasn't holding Alexis.

"Hey Chelsea. I'm still able to watch over everyone if you wanted to go back to sleep. I know you have Alexis with you, and she keeps on waking you up," I said.

My immediate reaction was to accept the offer and go back to sleep, if only to escape the boredom I was feeling, but I felt bad that it was Chelsea that would be up all by herself. My feelings of guilt were further exacerbated by the fact that she also had to take care of Alexis.

"It's okay, I don't mind. You need to rest as well. Anyhow," she continued, "I finally managed to get Alexis to fall asleep. She's cradled in between a bunch of bags, and a few sweaters. If I go lie down near her, she'll wake up. At least this way, I can make sure that she sleeps."

I nodded in agreement, but didn't make any move to go lay down. I wasn't really that tired anymore. Any inkling towards sleep that I was feeling, was solely due to being bored out of my mind.

"Chelsea, do you mind if I stay up with you? You know, to keep you company?" I asked her.

"Sure, no problem. The more the merrier. Are you sure you don't want to take this opportunity to sleep? Those two are out likes bricks. They won't be waking up anytime soon." She pointed towards the sleeping bodies of Samuel and Sarah.

"I'm sure," I replied.

I don't know if it was the complete darkness,

or the fact that everyone else was asleep, but I suddenly felt like confiding in her. Pulling out the letter that Rupert had written from my pocket, I unfolded it and handed it to her.

"I found this in my bag, when we were coming through the tunnel," I said. "The first time, with Samuel," I added, to clarify.

I watched as she read the letter. I tried to gage her reaction by studying her face, but her expression didn't change. When she finished reading the letter, she folded it back to how it was before, and handed it to me.

"I meant to tell you sooner, I swear. There just wasn't any other time I could find to talk to you about it. Samuel was always around, and that morning on the couch—"

Chelsea cut me off mid apology, and slung her arms around me, enveloping me in a semi embrace.

"Megan, relax. I'm not upset that you didn't tell me before. There's absolutely no reason for that at all. Although I do wish you had shown me sooner, so I could have dispelled any notions you may have and put your mind at ease sooner. Please do me a favour and don't pay any mind to that letter," she said.

"But Rupert wrote it. Isn't he your... I thought you would be on his side..." I didn't quite know what to think. Was she telling me that Samuel was innocent of any accusations Rupert was throwing at him? What did that say about Rupert? Was he a liar? Was he trying to throw me off on purpose?

"You haven't seen those two together as of yet, so it might be a little hard to wrap your head around," she began explaining. "I don't know exactly what happened, but those two have hated each other ever since Sam joined the Grover State Rebellion. Rupert has always had his suspicions about him, and he thinks he's not a trustworthy person.

"They've been at odds with each other since day one, and it's only getting worse. Rupert doesn't trust Sam one bit, and nothing you can say or do will ever change that reality, unfortunately.

"He tells everyone that Samuel can't be trusted, and to be wary of him. He's been trying very hard, especially these last couple of months, to prove that Sam's a mole working for Grover State."

"Is he?" I asked. "I mean, is Samuel a mole?"

Chelsea silently laughed at my question, and shook her head from side to side.

"I can guarantee you that Sam is no mole. He

has been at the forefront of most outbound missions—the most dangerous, might I add—since joining us. The only person who has completed more mission than him is Rupert. I trust him with my life, and with Alexis's life as well. He's a good person. He's an honest person. Don't let this letter make you treat him any differently."

I heaved a huge sigh of relief. Even though I hadn't really been thinking about it, the letter had been weighing heavy on my shoulders. It felt good to know that Samuel was a good guy, and that my first instincts were correct.

"But then, why would Rupert send me alone with Samuel to the safe house, if he thought he was dangerous?" I asked her, the question suddenly popping into my mind.

"He didn't have a choice in that. Sam is the only other person besides Sarah that can surgically remove identity chips. We couldn't afford to send Sarah into the state, and risk losing her. That's why she taught Sam the procedure in the first place. He's been the one responsible for most of the identity chip removals in all the ghostings we had completed. Oh, I don't know if Rupert or Sam explained that to you. Ghosting is when we, for a lack of a better word, kill people off the system. Everyone that lived at the safe house was a ghost," she explained.

"Yes, I think I remember them saying something about that. So, Samuel's a good guy, right?"

"Yes," she replied. "He's one of the best."

Chapter 23

I guess I must have fallen asleep sometime during the night. When I woke up, I could hear Sarah, Chelsea, and Samuel talking. I forced myself to become alert immediately, so as to not miss what they were saying.

"You can take those two bags there, and I can strap these ones on my back," Sam was saying to Chelsea, pointing towards two bags lying on the ground.

"But that will leave you carrying two bags along with Alexis. You carried three of them up until now. Take a break, and let me carry those three," Chelsea rebutted.

"It's okay, don't worry about it," Samuel said.

He quickly grabbed the bags before she could put up any further protest. Once the bags were safely and securely bound to his torso, he carefully grabbed Alexis from Chelsea's arms.

"Oh good, Megan's awake," Sarah said, as she noticed me. "We didn't want to wake you up."

"Thanks," I replied.

"Are we ready to go?" Sam asked.

I grabbed the two bags I was carrying, my original bag given to me by Rupert, and the one full of weapons I was carrying for Samuel, and stood beside him.

"We're as ready as we'll ever be," Sarah said.

Samuel began walking through the tunnel, with Alexis in tow. The three of us followed closely behind him. The rest break we had taken was worth the extra time added to our mission. I felt rejuvenated and ready to take on whatever might lay before us.

Samuel had reignited the orb light, and we walked in comfortable silence for a while. I looked around at everyone, and they all seemed focused on the task at hand. There were no longer any hints of smiles or laughter. Everyone was serious.

As we exited a tunnel section and entered the sewers once more, I tried to guess how far we were from arriving in Grover State. If I remembered correctly, we should only have about an hour left to go.

Everything was quiet when we all heard a noise coming from ahead of us. On what seemed to be sheer reflex alone, Samuel hid the light orb under his jacket, and we all remained frozen in silence. I was thankful that Alexis was quiet. She had been crying a mere fifteen minutes ago.

I couldn't see anything in the darkness, and the sound had disappeared. We all remained frozen in place, waiting to find out where the noise had come from.

"Are you guys okay?" Samuel whispered. "Do you see—"

Samuel's words were cut off, as he fell backwards. Since it was dark, I didn't properly judge his distance, and he sent me careening down to the floor with him. I tried to see what had made him fall down, but it was too dark.

I heard Chelsea or Sarah cry out, but I couldn't figure out why. I grasped for Samuel in the darkness, until my hands found his. I helped pull him up to his feet, as I got onto mine. As we stood up, the orb light fell out of his jacket, and the sewer was cast into light.

Standing before us was a Grover State police officer. We couldn't see his face because it was covered by a face shield, but I could tell it was a man due to the Adam's apple protruding from his throat.

We all stood frozen in silence, until a piercing cry was sounded from Alexis. Samuel looked down at

Alexis lying in his arms, and Chelsea turned around to look at her. That's when the police officer struck. He hit Samuel in the side of the head, which caused him to fall down on the floor.

Chelsea quickly reacted, and scooped up Alexis from his arms. Thankfully, he had managed to keep a steady hold on her as he fell to the ground. I was still frozen in place, and didn't realized that Chelsea was now standing right in front of me.

"Take Alexis. Run back down the sewers, just enough so that you can't get hurt. We'll keep him away from you and Alexis," she whispered in my ear, as she placed Alexis in my arms.

As soon as she was safely contained in my arms, I ran past all four of them, not taking the time to make out what was happening. My only concern was keeping Alexis alive.

I was now standing a few feet behind them. I was close enough to still see what was going on, but far enough so that I couldn't be attacked unless he got pass Sarah, Chelsea, and Samuel.

Samuel and Chelsea were both attacking the officer. The officer was trying to retrieve his weapon from his side pocket, but Chelsea was doing a really good job of blocking his access. Samuel swung multiple punches at him, and a few connected squarely with his face. However, that wasn't enough to stop him.

I noticed that Sarah had gone off to the side, and she was now riffling through one of the bags she was carrying. It was one of the bags filled with weapons, and she pulled out a long black gun. No one noticed her, as she aimed it at the officer.

I watched as Sarah pulled the trigger, but nothing happened. She fiddled with the gun for what seemed like an eternity, but was only truly a few seconds. She re-aimed the gun at the police officer, and pulled the trigger once more. This time, a loud sound erupted from the weapon. I didn't see what was ejected from the gun, but I saw its impact as the officer fell to the ground.

Instead of firing off another round, Sarah took the opportunity to rush him, using the weapon as a projectile. She hit him in the side of the head, and he fell back down to the ground. Sarah turned around to say something to Samuel, so she didn't notice as the officer quickly picked himself up off the ground.

"Sarah, behind you!" I shouted.

Sarah quickly turned around to see what I was referring to, but it was too late. The officer had managed to regain the advantage, and he struck Sarah with all his might. She was sent flying to the ground, falling backwards.

She struggled to get up, but he just kicked her under her chest, and she was thrown further backwards. Samuel and Chelsea rushed to her aid, but they weren't quick enough to prevent another blow being thrown at her.

Samuel jumped on his back, sending him crashing down to the ground. Sarah now had the opportunity to move and to escape his reach, but she just lay motionless on the ground.

Samuel was still holding firmly onto his back, which gave Chelsea the opportunity to pick up the weapon Sarah had dropped when the officer attacked her. Picking up the gun, she motioned at Samuel. He struggled with the officer, until he managed to get him in a position where his chest was fully exposed.

Chelsea fired off two more rounds from the gun, and they hit him right in the chest, where his heart should be. He continued struggling with Samuel still gripping tightly onto his back, until he fell to the ground motionless.

I was still frozen in place, watching the action before me. Chelsea dropped the weapon, and ran over to Sarah. I wasn't close enough to hear what she was saying to Samuel, but I could tell that Sarah wasn't moving.

As if I were snapping out of a reverie, I suddenly clued in on what was happening. The importance of it didn't dawn on me until just now. Sarah was lying on the ground, and she wasn't moving.

I ran over to Chelsea, still clutching Alexis tightly against my body. She was desperately trying to wake Sarah up. I felt a hand touch my shoulder, and turned around to see Samuel.

"Are you okay? Did you get hurt?" he asked me.

I shook my head to signal no, still too much in shock to open my mouth and answer.

I guess he realized that I wasn't in a position to coherently answer, so instead of asking me if Alexis was okay, he checked for himself. I felt my arms get lighter as the weight of Alexis was removed from them. Samuel quickly checked her to see if she was fine. He then placed her back in my arms, and went over to Sarah and Chelsea.

"Is she breathing?" Samuel asked Chelsea.

"Barely," she responded.

"Can you carry her bags? If you can manage, I should be able to carry her until we get to Amber and Tammy's."

"Yes, I should be able to manage."

Chelsea got up and retrieved the weapon, placing it back in its bag. She grabbed all of her bags, plus the two that Sarah had been carrying, and strapped them as comfortably as she could on her back. Samuel retook his bags, and picked up Sarah, supporting her in his arms. Her head was leaning against his shoulders, and her legs were swinging limply against his body.

I was left carrying Alexis, and remained frozen in place. There was an idea forming at the tip of my tongue, but I couldn't quite grasp it.

"Megan, are you coming?" Chelsea asked me.

"Wait," I said. "The officer." I pointed to the body lying on the ground, not sure if it was dead or merely unconscious.

"Don't worry. He's not going to follow us. He's dead," Samuel said.

"Oh," I said, mustering up the only response I could come up with.

"Okay, so can we go now?" Samuel asked me.

I could tell that he was trying to keep his voice

calm and stay patient with me. I wasn't doing it on purpose, but I couldn't shake myself out of the current state I was in. I tried once again to explain myself to him

"His clothes. Shouldn't one of us take his clothes, and dress up as a Grover State police officer? I mean, won't it help us get into the government building?" I asked.

I was looking at his face for feedback, but his expression didn't change. I didn't bother to look at Chelsea. I didn't want to risk seeing disappointment—or worse, anger—drawn on her face.

"That's brilliant Meg, quick thinking," Samuel said.

His praise somehow launched me out of my daze, and I was once again back to myself. Samuel carefully placed Sarah on the ground, resting her head on one of his bags.

"Don't worry, I'm not going to ask you to strip a corpse. I'll take the uniform off. Just watch over Sarah, and make sure that she's still breathing," he said.

Chelsea and I both watched as he crouched over the corpse of the police officer, and stripped off his uniform. I turned to face Sarah lying on the ground, and placed my ear against her chest. I could feel her chest rise and fall. She was still alive.

Once Samuel had managed to strip the officer of all his clothing and weapons, he stuffed all of the contents into one of the bags.

"Should we do something?" I asked. The corpse of the Grover State police officer was lying on the ground, almost nude. I felt bad just leaving the corpse like that. It felt wrong.

"We don't have time," Chelsea said, as she walked in front of Samuel to lead the way.

Samuel echoed the same sentiment, and made his way back to Sarah. He placed his bags back on his back, and scooped Sarah back into his arms. As soon as Sarah was comfortably balanced in his arms, he set forth to follow Chelsea. I followed closely behind, clutching Alexis against my chest. Glancing down at her briefly, I noticed that she was fast asleep.

Chapter 24

When we finally arrived at the tunnel opening that led into Tammy and Amber's apartment, we all heaved a huge sigh of relief. Samuel dropped all of his bags, and gently placed Sarah on the floor. Chelsea dropped her bags as well, and sat down with her back pressed against the wall.

"We made it," I said.

"Yes, we sure did. That was the easy part," Chelsea said.

She got up from the ground and made her way towards me. I angled Alexis towards her as I saw her approaching, figuring that she wanted to hold her baby. She picked her up from my arms, and kissed her forehead.

"What do we do now?" Chelsea asked Samuel.

"First things first, we need to take care of Sarah. She still hasn't woken up," he said.

"What about Alexis? We can't bring her with us anymore. What happened in the tunnel, that was too close. I don't know what would have happened if..." Chelsea's words trailed off, but both Samuel and

I knew what she was alluding to.

"Don't worry," Samuel reassured her. "We'll leave her with Amber and Tammy. She doesn't have an identity chip, so it shouldn't sound any alarms."

I could tell that Chelsea didn't like the prospect of leaving her child unattended, even if it was with two members of the Grover State Rebellion. Nonetheless, she nodded her agreement towards Samuel.

Samuel opened one of the bags he was carrying, and took out three cloaks.

"Do you still have the cloak Rupert gave you?" he asked me, as he put on one of the cloaks in his hands.

"Yes, it should be in my bag," I replied.

I opened my bag and was happy to see that my cloak was there, right where I had left it. Samuel handed a cloak to Chelsea who proceeded to put it on. Both her and Samuel helped each other as they placed the last cloak on Sarah's unconscious body.

"I'm going to go see Amber and Tammy. You guys stay down here until I come back down and give you the all clear. If you hear anything amiss, make a break for it through the tunnels. When you get far enough, release one of these." He handed a spherical grey canister to Chelsea, which fit in the palm of her hand. "Just make sure you throw it as far as possible. It will collapse the tunnel, but you'll be safe."

Chelsea placed the object that he had just handed her into her pocket, and we both watched as Samuel made his way up the ladder, and into the safe room.

Personally, I thought the best thing to do right now was to go into the safe room and place Sarah in the bed, but I wasn't the one in charge. They seemed to know what they were doing. And even if they didn't, I wouldn't know any better.

As I saw his feet disappear into the safe room, I turned my attention to Chelsea.

"Is she okay?" I asked, pointing at Alexis.

"I think so. She's still asleep. I didn't get a chance to tell you before, but thank you for protecting her," she said.

"It's not a big deal. You guys have been protecting me since this whole thing happened. I should be the one thanking you."

She flashed me one of her smiles, and it instantly warmed me up. I once again felt calm and collected.

"So," I began to ask, "what do we do now? I

mean, what do we do once Samuel comes back? Are we just going to go to the government building and..." I didn't bother finishing my sentence, because I had no idea what our new plan was, other than the basic detail-free outline we currently had.

"I'm not one hundred percent sure," she said, "because Samuel can change his mind in a split second, but we should be making our way to Rupert's. Once there, I imagine we'll start making our way towards the high priority neighbourhood and infiltrate the government building."

"What about Sarah? What if she doesn't wake up?"

"She'll wake up. She has to." The last sentence was more of a plea than a statement.

Chelsea was focusing her attention on Alexis. I think she was trying to spend as much quality time with her as possible, since we would soon be leaving her in the care of Tammy and Amber. I remained as quiet as possible, in an attempt to respect what she was doing.

Now that we had finally arrived in Grover State, I could feel the toll that the trip had physically taken on me. Unlike the first trip I had taken with Samuel, this one had been much harder on my body.

My body was physically tired, and was aching in places it never had, prior to today.

I started thinking back to the Grover State police officer that had attacked us in the tunnel. How did he know we would be there? Did someone tell him? Did the state know about the tunnel, or was he in there for some other reason?

"Chelsea, how did that officer get into the tunnel?" I asked her.

She planted a kiss on Alexis' forehead, before focusing her attention on me.

"I don't know," she replied. "Maybe he was just patrolling it."

"But, isn't the only way into the tunnel and sewers through here?" I asked.

I could see Chelsea's expression change before my very eyes to one of worry and concern. From the time we defeated the police officer, until we arrived at the tunnel's exit, this very realization hadn't dawned on any of us.

Chelsea carefully handed Alexis over to me, and kissed her once more on the forehead.

"Sam could very well be walking into a trap. I have to go and make sure he's okay. If anything happens, please take care of Alexis. Find Rupert and... Just, don't let anything happen to her," she said.

"I won't, I promise. I'll take care of her," I said. As the words came out of my mouth, I realized how true they were. If anything were to happen to them, I would take care of Alexis. There's no way I would let the state get their grubby hands on her.

Chelsea grabbed the ladder and made her way into the safe room. Once her feet disappeared from the opening, and the door was closed, I looked down at Alexis. She was now awake, but remarkably calm in my arms.

I walked over to where Sarah was lying on the floor, and sat down beside her. Her chest was rising with every breath she took, but she was still unconscious.

I was trying to figure out how I could save both of them, if someone came into the secret room. I wished Chelsea had left the weapon Samuel had given her, whatever it was called, with me. In the panic of things, she must have just forgotten.

Balancing Alexis in my hands, I fiddled with one of the bags full of weapons, and managed to open it one handed. I stuck my hand inside, and grabbed the smallest weapon I could find. Wrapping my hand around what felt like a gun, I pulled it out from the bag.

I found myself holding a small gun. I had no idea how to tell if it was loaded. I knew that it was used by pulling the trigger, but I wasn't sure if there was anything else I needed to do before that, to ensure that it functioned properly. No one from the Grover State Rebellion had had a chance to teach me how to operate weaponry.

Clutching the gun in my right hand, and cradling Alexis in my left, I focused my attention at the top of the ladder, where the door was firmly closed. I hoped that the gun was loaded and only needed to be triggered to work. Above that, I hoped that I wouldn't be presented with an opportunity where I had to use it. At least, not until Samuel or Chelsea could show me how to properly use a gun.

Chapter 25

I was still sitting near Sarah on the ground, holding onto Alexis in one arm, and the gun in the other. From time to time, I would check up on Sarah, but her status remained the same. I started to relax when all of a sudden, she started to stir. I immediately dropped the gun on the floor and focused my attention on her.

"Hey Sarah, are you okay? How do you feel?" I asked her.

She slowly opened her eyes, and took in her surroundings.

"Everything hurts, but I'll live," she said. She struggled to get up to a sitting position. I helped her as best as I could, but it was hard since I was still holding on to Alexis.

"Where are we?" she asked.

"The entrance to the tunnel. We're in the room under Amber and Tammy's safe room," I answered.

"Where's everybody? Where's Sam? Where's Chelsea? Did... did that police officer get them? Are we the only ones left?"

"No, no. Samuel and Chelsea went up to go talk to Amber and Tammy. They thought it would be best for us to stay down her, in case anything happened."

I didn't have the heart to tell her that Chelsea had gone to check up on Samuel, for fear that he was walking into a trap. I still hadn't heard from any of them, and they had been gone for at least twenty minutes.

I watched as she propped herself to her feet, and walked around to loosen up her limbs. I noticed that she was limping a bit, but otherwise she seemed okay. I was relieved that she was finally awake. When Samuel and Chelsea came back—and I was confident that they would—they would be happy to see that Sarah had regained consciousness.

After she sufficiently stretched out her legs, she came back towards me and motioned for me to give her Alexis. I extended her towards her outreached arms, and she gently cradled her against her chest.

"I'm glad that she's safe and that nothing happened to her," she said, as she kissed the baby's forehead.

I was slightly astounded to the amount of care and love they all showed towards one another. The love and care they showed towards Alexis, who was in no way shape or form their responsibility, was more than a citizen of Grover State showed towards children appointed to them. My parents had loved me, and I knew that behind hidden doors they expressed that love more than what was tolerated by the state. But this was different. It gave me hope.

"So, what did I miss while I was knocked out?" Sarah asked me.

"Not much," I replied. "Samuel and Chelsea killed the police officer. We took his clothes, and Samuel carried you here. And then they both went up. Samuel first, and then Chelsea followed him."

"How long have they been gone for?" she asked.

I was hesitant to tell her the truth, because I didn't want her to think that something might have happened. Samuel and Chelsea had been gone for a while, but it could be for a multitude of reasons that didn't involve any negative consequences.

"Megan, how long?" she asked me again. This time, her voice was more forceful.

"Twenty minutes. Maybe half an hour. I'm not

sure, I don't know what time it is," I spat out.

"Okay," she said, as she calmed back down. I was surprised. I thought she was going to start panicking and fly up that ladder to go and find them. I guess half an hour wasn't that long according to their standards.

I got up off the ground, picking up the gun as I did. Extending it towards Sarah, I asked her if she could show me how to use it.

"Sure," she said. "I'm surprised no one has shown you by now. I'll have to have a talk with those two. I can't believe all this time has passed, and they still haven't shown you basic weapon skills."

I nodded my head and silently agreed with her. I was a bit upset that no one had taken the time to teach me how to fire a gun. I was a member of the Grover State Rebellion, after all.

Sarah carefully placed Alexis on two of the bags not holding any weapons, so that she was comfortably propped above the ground. She then dragged one of the bags full of weapons in front of her, and opened it up.

"It's really easy," she said. "For most of these guns, all you have to do is pull the trigger. There's no safety on any of these. Almost all of the weapons we have are standard Grover State military issue, and none of their weapons have safeties."

I eagerly listened to her, taking in all the information she was teaching me. Learning like this was a drastic change from all the previous learning I had done in the Education Room. Instead of having to read a text on how to use the weapons, she was showing me.

After she showed me how to load and reload the chambers in all the different guns we had, she showed me where the extra ammunition was kept. It was in one of the bags Samuel had been carrying.

"Aim for the centre whenever you shoot. Don't try to hit the head or any limbs. No offense, but you're more than likely to miss. Also, be very careful. There's no safety on any of the guns, so they can go off at a moment's notice. Don't carry any of those hidden on your body, unless you're about to shoot them," Sarah said.

She removed a gun that was tucked in her waistband and handed it to me. "This one is mine. It has a safety. You just remove it like this." She took the gun and showed me how to remove the safety, and handed it back to me. "You can keep this one, I have another one. You reload it the same as the others. I personally modified it. It will accept and shoot any bullets in that bag." She pointed to the bag filled with ammo.

"Thank you," I said to her, as I turned the gun over in my hands, examining it.

I tucked the gun into my waistband, just as she had. It wasn't much, but I felt much more empowered than I had before. If someone other than a Grover State Rebellion member came through that door and down the ladder, I was confident I could protect us. Well, I was confident that I could help Sarah protect us.

I walked over to where Alexis was laying down, and found her fast asleep. I was about to pick her up, but decided against it. The last thing I wanted was to have her start crying, and be the reason why someone finds us down here.

"Megan, can you stay here for a moment," Sarah asked me.

"You're going to go look for Samuel and Chelsea?" I asked her.

"Yes," she responded, not needing to elaborate.

"Can I come with you?" I asked her. I didn't want to stay here, sitting down and doing nothing at all while everyone else risked their lives.

"What about Alexis?" she retorted. "Someone needs to watch her."

I was upset that I couldn't go with her, but I didn't really have much else to say. She was right; someone needed to stay with Alexis. Between the two of us, I was the obvious choice to stay behind. If Samuel and Chelsea were truly in danger, than she would be much better suited at helping them.

I watched as she made her way to the base of the ladder, and grabbed onto the rung directly in front of her. As soon as she placed her foot on the bottom rung, the door to the hidden room opened.

Sarah quickly stepped away from the ladder and grabbed her gun from her waistband, identical to the one she had given me. I did the same, remembering to remove the safety mechanism first. We both aimed our guns at the top of the ladder, and waited for someone to come down.

Someone started descending the ladder, but I couldn't quite tell who it was yet. After their head was visible, Sarah and I both let out a sigh of relief. Chelsea was coming down the ladder, and back into the room.

As soon as Chelsea's feet hit the ground, she

turned around to face us and motioned for us to be quiet. At the same time, a large smile spread across her face as she realized that Sarah had finally woken up.

"How are you feeling?" Chelsea whispered to Sarah.

"I've been better, but I'm still alive," Sarah whispered back.

They both hugged each other in a tight embrace. When they finally let go of each other, Chelsea looked around for Alexis. When she spotted her, she walked over to where she was lying and picked her up. She made her way back towards us, and filled us in on what was going on.

"Sam's up in the safe room," she explained in a whisper. "As far as we can tell, the safe room is somewhat secure. As for the rest of the unit, well... I didn't see anything first hand, but Sam said that there were two Grover State police officers in the living room. As soon as he spotted them, he returned to the safe room.

"I don't think they know about the safe room, because nothing has been moved and the two officers haven't made any attempt to come in yet. From the little that Sam was able to see, the place was ransacked. He was able to spot the digital display near the door, and it read two occupants."

Chelsea paused, and looked at each of us with a hint of sadness. Even I knew what that meant: Amber and Tammy were not in the apartment. They were most likely captured, and detained just like the rest of the Grover State Rebellion members.

"We still don't know how that police officer managed to get into the tunnel. They clearly don't know how to access the safe room, although Sam seemed pretty convinced that they are aware of it; they just don't seem to know how to access it.

"Sam has been checking on them, just so that we know where they are. As soon as the digital display reads zero, we have to leave. We don't know how long it will be until they figure out how to get into the safe room, so we have the leave at the first opportunity we have.

"We have to stay quiet until they're gone. As long as we can do that, the only thing we have to worry about is Alexis. Thankfully, she's sleeping right now. I'll do my best to keep her quiet. The sound barrier in the safe room should block out any noise, but I don't want to take a chance."

After she finished talking, she went back up

the ladder with Alexis in tow. Sarah grabbed all of the bags that she could manage, and followed closely behind. I picked up the remaining bags that were lying on the floor, and followed suit.

As soon as my head popped through the opening in the floor, I felt a bunch of hands grabbing me to help me up. Once I was completely out of the hidden room below, Chelsea quietly closed the door. The bags that were strapped on me were really heavy, so I carefully placed them on the floor.

Sam was in front of the door to the safe room, with his ear pressed against it. He hadn't made a single movement or other indication to acknowledge my presence. For some reason it hurt me emotionally, but I quickly pushed the feelings away. There would be time for that when we weren't trying to figure out how to survive.

"As soon as Sam gives us the go ahead," Chelsea whispered, "we're going to leave and make a break for it to Rupert's. It's already past curfew, so the only thing we'll have to worry about is the state police. As long as we stay together and out of sight, we should be able to evade them."

"But what if the state police have already gotten to Rupert's unit, and are lying in wait for us?

Won't we just be walking into a trap? We won't have the safety of the safe room like we do now," Sarah asked Chelsea.

"Unfortunately, we don't really have the luxury of choice. Once we get there, we'll deal with it then. There's one thing I'm certain of, and that's that we can't stay here and expect any amount of safety. We might as well move forward."

Sarah nodded her head, while I remained silent watching the exchange between the two. I had no input, nor did I feel the inclination to have any. I would go wherever the group went. We were in this together.

Chapter 26

We had been waiting in silence for a few hours now. Luckily for us, Alexis had remained quiet so far. She was now awake, but she merely cooed every so often. Chelsea had made sure to feed and change her as soon as she seemed to want it. So far, her instincts had been correct.

Samuel had been sneaking in and out of the safe room, checking up on the location of the state police. They stayed in the living room the entire time, except for once when Rupert saw them in the kitchen. Although they never seemed to stray into the hallway, Samuel was convinced that they were looking for the hidden access to the safe room.

All four of us were prepared to leave at a moment's notice, which is what we were currently set up to do. Chelsea and Sarah went around the safe room and collected a few things that they thought might be useful, in case we weren't able to come back here. Chances were, as long as Grover State was in power and on our trail, once we left we would never be able to return and expect any reasonable amount of safety.

Sam had just left for another check, and came back running into the safe room. This time, he had been gone longer than usual. He grabbed his bags that were set by the door, and turned around to address us, no longer bothering to whisper.

"They're gone. I double checked, and there's no sign of them. The hallway and staircase seem clear. I scanned the area, and there are not police officers nearby. Well, at least none that show on their system.

"We have to leave now. We don't have time to wait and see. Chances are we're safe to go to Rupert's, but we're still taking chances. Are you all good to go now? Any objections?" Samuel asked.

We all shook our heads to indicate we didn't have any objections with the plan. We had been waiting for hours to leave, not moving from the room. It would be a welcome change to be outside in the fresh air.

All of a sudden, Samuel dropped his bags back to the floor as he rummaged through one of them. We all watched as he stripped off his clothing, and put on the Grover State Police uniform.

"Just in case," he said, as he put the face

shield in place.

Samuel led the group outside the safe house, and we followed behind. Now that I had a chance to see it myself, I could see how they turned the place upside down. Most of the furniture was broken by force, and the floor was littered with everything that once had a home in a drawer, on a table, or in a box.

I had meant to ask Samuel if there was a chance that Amber and Tammy were still in the apartment hiding somewhere, but I knew it was pointless. In the short amount of time that I've known him, there's one thing I know for sure: the first thing he would have done, once the unit was clear of the police officers, would have been to look for them.

We went through the hallway without incident, and eventually went out the building the same way Samuel and I had originally come in. As soon as the cool air touched my skin, I rejoiced inside. Amidst all this chaos, something as small as fresh air after being cooped up indoor, whether it be the tunnel or the unit, was refreshing.

The moon was shining brightly in the sky, but there was no time to stop and admire it. Hopefully, if everything went according to plan, there would be plenty more of them in my future.

Sarah was still in pain, but she was trying her very best to hide it. I caught her limping a few times, and even offered to lend her a helping hand with her bags. She refused, but I didn't really understand why. Clearly, she needed help.

On two occasions, Samuel made us all stop so that Sarah could take a break. The first time, when Samuel indicated that we were stopping for her, she made a huge fuss and insisted we continue to Rupert's, despite her aggressive limp and looks of pain drawn on her face. The second time we stopped, having learned his lesson the first time, he feigned concern over Alexis so that she wouldn't know we were stopping for her.

Once we arrived in the mid priority area, a bunch of feelings rushed through my body. I was seeing things that had been part of my life, up until recently. Upon arriving at Rupert's building block— my old building block—something inside of me stirred and caused my heart rate to accelerate.

We carefully snuck into the building, and made our way to Rupert's unit. Curiosity snuck up on me, and I suddenly had a deep desire to revisit my old unit. I wondered if the Grover State Police had ransacked it as well. Did they know I wasn't really dead? I guess only time would tell.

As we passed through the hallway, I resisted asking the group to stop. That was the last thing we needed, and there was nothing there that would be of use to us.

Standing in front of Rupert's door, Samuel motioned for us to stand to the side. We all exchanged looks of concern when we simultaneously noticed that the digital display near the door read zero occupants.

Samuel took out a device from his pocket and waved it in front of the door. The door slowly opened, and we all followed him inside. I was bringing in the rear of the group, so I was the last to understand why Chelsea let out a small cry, that she quickly stifled.

The apartment was ransacked, far worse than Amber and Tammy's had been. Everything that could be destroyed was. Even the light fixtures were broken, with some barely hanging by their wires. It all looked horrible, but the worst was lying in a puddle on the floor, where Chelsea was currently kneeling, desperately trying not to cry. On the floor in front of her was what I could only assume to be Rupert's blood.

Sarah and Samuel went over to Chelsea to try to comfort her. Samuel grabbed Alexis from her arms, and Sarah knelt down beside her.

"We're too late," Chelsea sobbed. "He's...he's..."

"We don't know that for sure. The state police could have detained him. He could be with the others, and we'll save him when we save them," Sarah tried to reassure her.

"Why would there be blood, if all they did was detain him?" she asked through sobs.

Sarah didn't say anything. She just wrapped her arms around Chelsea, and held her tightly. We all knew what the blood meant; there had been no blood at Amber and Tammy's.

I stood frozen in place, watching Sarah console Chelsea. Samuel was still holding onto Alexis. It looked like he was trying to figure out what to do.

All of a sudden, we heard a noise coming from the hallway. Samuel ducked down and shielded Alexis, while Sarah pulled out her gun and aimed it in the direction of the noise. I clumsily fumbled for my gun, and dropped it on the floor. As I bent down to pick it up, I heard Chelsea squealing. Scared that something had happened to her, I quickly picked up my gun and stood up.

As soon as I saw why Chelsea had been squealing, I placed my revolver back in my waistband. She was hugging Rupert. An alive Rupert. He was battered and bruised, but he seemed okay.

We all took turned hugging him. Once he got to Samuel, he picked up Alexis and squeezed her tightly against his chest, laying multiple kisses on top of her head and on her forehead.

Chapter 27

"I'm so glad you guys are okay, but why are you here? What happened?" Rupert asked, addressing no one in particular.

"They found us. I don't know how, but they found us. Megan and I got attacked as we were coming back from foraging. Two Grover State military soldiers ambushed us and attacked. If it wasn't for Sam, I don't know if we'd be standing here right now," Sarah said.

"What about the others?" Rupert asked. "Are they still at the safe house?"

No one answered. We all looked at Samuel, and he sighed before addressing Rupert. "They were gone by the time that I was able to go back and help them. I checked everywhere, and there was no trace of them. I'm pretty sure they're being detained right now, probably in re-education."

We all looked at Rupert to gage his reaction, but his expression didn't change.

"We came through the tunnel, and we were attacked by a police officer. He beat on Sarah pretty badly, but she's still alive and kicking," Samuel said, as he pointed towards her. "Amber and Tammy... I don't know how to say this, but they're gone too. Their apartment is in shambles. Not to this extent, but pretty much the same basic idea."

Rupert still remained quiet. Samuel kept on filling him in on things he had forgotten to say before. Once he recounted every minute detail and Rupert still remained quiet, it became very awkward. Rupert looked angry. Finally turning his head towards Samuel to address him, he opened his mouth and spoke.

"How exactly did the Grover State police know how to find us. There's no way that they could have known about the tunnel, unless someone told them," Rupert said, through gritted teeth.

Samuel grabbed his arm, trying to lead him back through the hallway. "I understand your question, Rupert, but let's get to the safe room first. They could be listening to us right now. You're not holding onto a scrambler. Your identity chip... Did you forget?"

Rupert must have taken offence at what Samuel said to him, because he pulled his arm away from him and took a step back.

"No, I did not forget," he spat out.

We all watched as Rupert lifted up his shirt sleeve, revealing a bandaged wound. He had removed his identity chip. He was still holding onto Alexis, and she started crying at the sudden movement.

"It's okay, Alexis. Shh, it's okay. Here, go see mommy," he said, as he handed her to Chelsea. Chelsea quickly grabbed Alexis and worked on calming her down.

"I don't know what your problem is, but we don't have time for this," Samuel said to Rupert.

By now, Sarah and I had migrated to stand beside Chelsea. We had no intentions of being caught in the middle of their squabble.

"I don't know, why don't you tell me. How exactly did they know where the safe house was? Or Amber and Tammy's? Or my unit? Tell me, Sam, how did they know?" Rupert was in Samuel's face, yelling as much as humanly possible at a low volume barely above a whisper.

"Well, it wasn't me, if that's what you're thinking," he retorted.

Before any of us could anticipate it, Rupert swung his arm back and leaned all his weight into a punch aimed at Samuel's head. Samuel was able to dodge the blow to his head, but it still caught him on his shoulder.

There were no longer any words being exchanged between the two. Rupert and Samuel were fighting, trading blow for blow. Whenever one of them would get knocked down to the ground, they would bounce back up before you knew it.

Rupert had managed to get on top of Samuel, and he straddled his chest as he lay punch after punch into him. Samuel shifted his weight, which caused Rupert to lose his balance and fall. Samuel took the opportunity to gain the advantage over him. Samuel was now straddling him in the exact same position, hitting him repeatedly in the face.

Chelsea handed Alexis over to Sarah, and ran to where they were fighting. As Samuel was throwing another punch at Rupert, she caught his fist midair.

"Okay, you've had your fun. Now stop it. There's no need for them to hunt us down, when we're just doing their job for them," she said to both men.

As she let go of Samuel's fist, he reluctantly got off of Rupert. Rupert immediately got back up, and lunged towards him. Chelsea placed herself between both men, and pushed them apart.

"Enough. Sam, Rupert... give it a rest," she said.

Rupert and Samuel were both breathing and heaving pretty heavily, but they stopped lunging after each other. Chelsea removed herself from in between the two of them. They were still staring each other down, but they weren't touching each other anymore.

"Are you guys done now?" Chelsea asked.

"Why don't you ask your little Grover State spy here," Rupert retorted, not once wavering his eyes from Samuel.

"For the last time, I'm not a spy. I do not work for Grover State. I'm part of the Grover State Rebellion too, or did you forget," Samuel replied.

"Well, if it's not you, then who is it?" Rupert asked him.

"I don't know. But hell, you've got to lay off of me. I'm not automatically the bad guy, just because you can't label anyone else," Samuel said.

"I said enough," Chelsea repeated.

Both Samuel and Rupert stopped talking, but they were still throwing each other dirty looks.

"We don't have time for any of this. I don't know if you remember, but more than half of our group is currently being held against their will. Just try to imagine the pain and torture they must be under right now. Got it? Good," she said to Samuel and Rupert.

"Okay, we all need to rest and recuperate. Rupert, is it safe for us to stay in the safe room tonight?" she asked.

"Yes, they haven't found it. They don't know it's here," he replied, in a softer tone than he had been using prior.

"Good. We're all going to go lay down and rest, and get ready for tomorrow. We need to be well rested if we're going to be of any help to anyone. Do you think you can both behave, or should we just surrender ourselves to the state right now?" Chelsea asked, still addressing the two men.

"Don't look at me," Samuel said. "He's the one that attacked me."

"Rupert?" she asked.

"Yes, sure, whatever," he replied.

Rupert gently grabbed Alexis from Sarah, and led us all into the safe room. Chelsea, Rupert, and Alexis got the bed. The rest of us roughed it out on the floor. Closing my eyes as I slowly drifted into sleep, I silently hoped that Rupert and Samuel wouldn't attack each other while we all slept.

Chapter 28

The next morning when I woke up, everything was back to normal. Samuel and Rupert weren't as friendly as when I first met them together, but they were cordial. I wasn't entirely sure, but something told me he was only keeping his calm because of Chelsea.

We had unanimously decided to go into the city centre, located in the high priority neighbourhood, tonight after curfew. By now I was getting tired of eating the MGNS, and the novelty of a pill turning into water had worn off on me. Well, at least we had food and water.

Rupert and Sarah spent a few hours training me in weapons combat. Sarah wanted to teach me how to fight without any weapons, but Rupert said that I wasn't ready for that yet. She ignored him, and trained me anyways.

Sarah taught me basic self defence skills, and a few combat moves to use in case someone attacked me. She told me to not resort to hand to hand combat unless absolutely necessary. I was directed to always stay between two of them, so that I could not be cornered.

I was busy putting my bag together when I heard everyone start to argue. I kept my head down, still focused on my bag, while straining to hear what was going on.

"I don't understand why I should stay behind," Sarah said. "Megan has no combat experience. She's the most logical choice to stay behind with Alexis."

"Come on, Sarah. Face facts. You can barely walk, and I can tell you're in constant pain. You limped most of the way here. You were unconscious for how long? You're in no condition to fight," Chelsea said.

"She's right," Rupert added. "The safest place for you right now is here. Megan will do just fine. If we're lucky, we won't have to get into much combat."

"I can still fight. You can't just write me out of the plan," she said.

"We can't risk losing you. Please, I'm begging you. Plus, you can protect Alexis. In case anything happens to us, we'll know she'll be safe with you. Please?" Rupert pleaded.

Sarah reluctantly agreed, and the argument

was put to rest. I was so distracted by their conversation that I had inadvertently removed all the contents from my bag, in an attempt to fit in what I would need for tonight. I started putting everything back in, when I noticed the black metal box I had taken from the military base.

"What's that?" I heard Samuel ask above me.

I glanced up to look at him, and told him where it had come from. I handed it to him, and he examined it. He didn't know what it was, but was deeply intrigued. Rupert happened to glance over, and noticed that Samuel was holding it. He came over and swiped the box from him.

"Hey, what do you think you're doing? I was looking at that," Samuel said to Rupert.

"Just be quiet for a second. Where did you get this from?" he asked.

"Megan found it in a mobile military base that they erected close to the safe house. I'm not sure what it is though," he replied.

"I know what it is," Rupert said. "Chelsea, Sarah, come here. I think I just figured out how we're going to win." A smile spread across his face.

Sarah and Chelsea came over to where we were, and we all patiently waited for Rupert to tell us what he meant. He was rotating the box in his hands, admiring it with delight.

"Do you know what this is? It's a memory block that was built by Grover himself. I mean, the original Grover. It's the master key for the entire system. It contains every single string of code used to run the state. It also contains the code for its destruction. If I'm not mistaken, all we need to do is plug it into the system's core, and the memory block will do the rest," he said.

"Are you sure? How do you know that that's the memory block built by Grover? Why would they leave it there, in plain sight?" Samuel asked.

"I don't know, but I'm sure that it's the one made by Grover. All we need to do is plug this into the system's core, and it will corrupt the system's software, leading it to self-destruct. We can sit back, and watch as everything that relies on the state's network goes offline. Grover State will be no more," he said.

No one spoke for a while, as we all let Rupert's words sink in. I never would have imagined, not in a million years, that I would be the one to find the key that would destroy Grover State.

"So," Sarah spoke up, "I guess that means the

plan has changed?"

"Yes and no," Rupert said. "You're still going to stay here with Sarah. We're still going to break into the containment centre and free everyone that's been detained. And I'm talking about everyone. Not just Grover State Rebellion members, but every single person that the state has detained.

"We'll use the cover of that commotion to find the central system that controls all of this, and we'll stick this in to finish the job." Rupert raised the memory block in front of his face, so that it was prominently displayed.

"Okay then," Chelsea said. "Let's go get ready. It's almost curfew."

*****

As soon as curfew hit, we were ready to leave. Chelsea and Rupert both kissed Alexis goodbye, and we all hugged Sarah. Samuel changed out of the Grover State Police uniform he was wearing, preferring to wage war in his own clothing. I was excited and nervous at the same time. I was afraid of everything that might go wrong, but also hopeful of everything that might go right.

Rupert took the lead, and Samuel brought up the rear. We all walked in silence, careful to steer clear of any state police officers that might be patrolling the streets.

Rupert said that he knew how to get to the high priority neighbourhood without being detected. I had never been there in my life, so I was curious to see how that area differentiated from mine. Well, not mine. I wasn't a citizen anymore.

I was so focused on concentrating on the others, that I didn't notice when our scenery had changed. We must have arrived in the high priority neighbourhood, because it was beautiful. Even though everything was cast in the darkness of night, I could still make out all the vibrant colours in the multiple gardens surrounding us. The housing blocks looked magnificent. Although the low and mid priority housing blocks differed, they still had many similar features. The ones here were in a class of their own.

I didn't recognize the majority of the things we came across, but that didn't really matter; my focus was elsewhere.

All of a sudden, Rupert stopped walking, and we all came to a grinding halt behind him. He took out something from his pocket, and waived it in front of him. After a few minutes of painstaking silence, he slipped it back into his pocket.

"We should be clear to go. It's after curfew, so there shouldn't be anyone in the building. Make sure you keep your cloaks on, or else the system will pick something up. Are you guys ready?" Rupert asked us.

"Are you sure that it's safe to just go in there? What if you're wrong, and the place is crowded with police officers. The military bases aren't too far from here. That's a possibility too," Samuel said.

"Trust me, I've broken into here before. How do you think I knew about the memory block? Come on, we have to hurry," he said.

Rupert led us through a side door in the building. We walked up and down countless staircases, and hallways. When we finally arrived at a door labelled CONTAINMENT CENTER, I thought it must have truly been a miracle that we hadn't been caught. We hadn't even seen a single police officer.

"Are you guys ready?" Rupert asked.

As we all nodded our heads, he gently opened the door and led us through. We walked inside and were face to face with a large glass room, filled with people. I peered inside and recognized a few members of the Grover State Rebellion that had been at the safe house.

All of a sudden, my jaw fell wide open. I couldn't tell due to my current state, but I was pretty sure everyone else was having a similar reaction. Staring directly at me from the containment chamber were my parents.

Chapter 29

"Lucas? Amanda? Is that really them?" Rupert asked, in disbelief.

I couldn't contain my own excitement. I ran to the glass separating us, and lay my hand against the glass. My parents flashed me a warm smile. My insides felt as if they were warming up to dangerous temperatures; I was experiencing feelings I had never felt before.

"How do we get them out of there?" I asked Rupert.

"I'm not sure, but we'll figure it out," he said.

I watched as Rupert fiddled with the lone computer that was in the room. He kept on hitting a bunch of different sequences, but nothing happened. Samuel and Chelsea were guarding the door, weapons aimed at the ready.

I heard someone walking behind me, and assumed it was either Chelsea or Samuel. I turned around to see why they had left their positions, and let out a cry that got Rupert's attention. Standing before me was Edward Grover, the leader of Grover

State.

"We finally meet. You're the Grover State Rebellion? Hum. For some reason, I pictured your group as being larger. Easier for me, I guess," he said.

I was frozen in place; I couldn't even move an inch as he was approaching towards me. I couldn't see him, but I assumed Rupert was in a similar position to mine.

"Did you think that it would be that easy for you to waltz in here? Who do you think I am? You do know who I am, do you not?" he asked no one in particular.

He approached me until he was standing face to face with me. I could feel his stale breath on my face. As he stared me down, I blinked and averted my eyes.

He continued walking towards Rupert. I was too scared to move from my position. I could finally see a glimpse of Chelsea and Samuel, and they were frozen in place as well. While it didn't make me feel any better about our predicament, it felt comforting to know that they felt just as I did.

"Let me guess," Grover continued. "You came here to rescue your little merry band of deviants? Now, I'm not one for theatrics. I could kill you on the spot if I wanted to. But I'm not going to. Do you know why?"

When no one answered, he slammed his hand against the wall and bellowed: "I asked you a question! You will show me the proper respect and answer me!"

"I don't know," Rupert said. I could hear the gulp that he took as he answered.

"Let me tell you why," Grover said, his voice back to normal. "You have something that I want. I could attack you and retrieve it myself, but I don't feel like wasting my manpower on you. I am here to offer you a proposition. Give me the memory block, and I will let you walk away."

Rupert's bravado returned. He stood to his full height, and addressed Grover. "Why would you let us just walk away?"

"It's simple, really. I have no use for you. No amount of rehabilitation will correct your thinking now. You can go back and live—if that's what you call it—out there. It's only a matter of time until the elements eventually get you. I will allow you to escape through those wretched sewers that you think I don't know about, and then I will fill them with cement," he said.

"Why should we believe you?" Rupert asked.

"What other choice do you have?"

Rupert seemed to be thinking over what he had said. I was still too scared to move. I was just waiting for one of them to speak.

"What about the others?" Rupert asked.

"You can have them. But only them."

"Amanda and Lucas too?"

"If you want those traitors, go ahead," he sneered.

I was so focused on their back and forth conversation, that I didn't realize when Rupert started addressing me.

"Megan!" Rupert called out.

I looked at Rupert, my focus now solely on him. I locked eyes with him. I was still too frozen to speak. Luckily for me, I didn't need to.

"Megan, give him the memory block," Rupert directed me.

Not removing my eyes from him, I removed my bag from my back and opened it. I plunged my hand inside and felt around until I brushed against the metal box, the memory block. I removed it from the bag and extended it towards Grover.

"Bring it to me," Grover directed.

I quickly ran forward and handed him the memory block. As soon as his hands grasped it, I ran to stand beside Rupert. He examined it for a bit, and then made his way to where we were standing, in front of the computer.

"Do you mind?" Grover asked. It was more of a statement than a question.

We moved from the computer, and watched as Grover typed in a sequence. In a matter of seconds, the glass that was separating us from the containment chamber opened up.

"You know who you are. Step out," Grover directed.

One by one, the members of the Grover State Rebellion stepped forward and exited the chamber. My dad was the last one to come out. As soon as he came out, Grover immediately entered another sequence into the computer to close the glass divider.

Even though we were standing on the edge of death, I didn't care. As soon as I saw both of my parents, alive and well standing in front of me, I ran into their arms. They both embraced me, and I felt on top of the world. At that moment, it didn't matter that these might be my last few minutes alive.

"So, are we free to leave?" Rupert asked.

"In time, in time," Grover said.

"Are you going to let us go, or not?" Rupert asked again, this time more forcefully. "Either kill us where we stand, or let us go."

"How dare you speak to me with such indignity? You will do what I say, and when I say. Have I made myself clear?" Grover said to Rupert.

"You're nothing but a liar. Grover State is a lie. We're not the only ones alive. There's something out there, and no matter how bad it may be, it's a million times better than this," he replied.

Grover slammed his hands on the computer in front of him, causing the monitor to crash down to the floor. His face was flushed red, and he was starting to shake.

"How dare you? You...you..." Grover's words tapered off. His face contorted in shock as he grabbed a hold of the table in front of him.

No one spoke, as we watched Edward Grover, the founding image of Grover State, collapse onto the floor. Blood starting pooling around his body. He was dead.

"Who...?" Rupert began to ask, as he tried to figure out what had happened.

I looked around the room, and saw Chelsea

holding her gun, still aimed where Grover's standing body had been. She slowly lowered the gun to her side, and tucked it back into her waistband.

"I guess we're free to go now," she said.

The mood in the room suddenly changed. Could it actually be true? Had we won? Everyone had smiles on their faces. Rupert had picked up the computer monitor from the floor, and placed it back on the desk. It looked like he was trying to figure out how to open the glass partition, in order to let everyone else out.

Chelsea walked over to Edward Grover's dead body, and knelt down over it. I wasn't sure what she was doing, until I saw her pick up the memory block that had fallen to the ground beside him.

I was still standing with my parents, beaming from ear to ear. I don't think I could have imagined a better outcome. Not only had we defeated Edward Grover, but my parents were alive.

"Guys, we still need to figure out how to put this into the system's core, to override the system," Chelsea announced to everyone, waving the memory block in her hands.

I heard my dad speak behind me. I looked at him as he addressed Chelsea. The sound of his voice caused my heart to jump against my chest. He was really alive. And so was my mom.

"We don't have any protection. Did you bring any extra weapons?" he asked.

"Yes, we have a bag full. Here, take my pistol," Chelsea answered.

She removed her gun from her waistband, and handed it to my dad. I could see Samuel rummaging through the bag of weapons. He grabbed two guns and walked towards us. He gave one gun to Chelsea, to replace the one she had given my dad, and the other to my mom.

"Can I see that for a moment?" my dad asked Chelsea, pointing at the gun Samuel had just handed her.

Everything happened so fast, that I wasn't entirely sure of what I was seeing. No, that's not true. I knew what I was seeing, but I didn't want to believe it.

As Chelsea obliged and gave my dad her gun, he hit Samuel with the butt of it. And then, just as quickly, he pointed the gun at Chelsea.

"Give me the memory block," he said to her.

"What the hell, Lucas? Have you lost your mind? What are you doing?" Chelsea asked, in disbelief.

Her outburst caused Rupert to look away from the computer screen. As soon as he saw a gun pointed at Chelsea, he rushed to her aid. Before he could get close enough to be of any help, my mom pointed her gun at him.

"So you're the rat, huh," Rupert said to them. "I should have known."

"Don't kid yourself, Rupert. You had no idea until just now," my mom said.

"When did you guys turn? What did they threaten you with?" Rupert asked.

"What misconceptions you have," my dad said. "We never turned. We were always loyal to our beloved Grover State. As you can tell, we've succeeded in our mission. What was it again, Amanda?"

"To seek and destroy the Grover State Rebellion from within," my mom answered.

"Ah, yes," my dad continued. "I would say that we've achieved our goal."

"Then why were you two locked up with the rest of the group," Chelsea asked.

"The state found out about our plans of betrayal. We planned on double-crossing them. If everything had gone according to plan, I was going to have my face surgically altered to resemble our dear leader here, and take over," he said.

"Yeah, we know. That was our plan," Chelsea retorted.

"No, it was part of the plan. A plan that I came up with, if you remember correctly. The part you're missing, the most crucial one of all, is the part where we kill all of you and take full control over the state. We had no intentions of destroying Grover State. As far as we're concerned, this is as good as it gets. We're in charge now. By the way, I forgot to thank you for taking out Edward. You saved us the trouble," my dad said.

I couldn't believe what I was hearing. How could my parents betray us like that? How could they betray me?

"Mom? Dad?" I didn't know what else to say.

"Ah, Megan. You played your role very nicely. Without you, we never would have been able to lead the military to the safe house. I knew I could count on Rupert to take you there," he said.

"You used your own daughter as a pawn?" Rupert shouted to my dad.

"She is not of my blood. There is no loyalty.

She is no more mine than she is yours," he replied.

I couldn't believe what I was hearing. Tears were streaming down my face, blurring my vision. The words that were coming out of my dad's mouth: they couldn't be real. But they were.

"Mom?" I managed to get out, looking for solace.

But, none came.

"Oh, just shut up," she said to me.

The tears continued running down my face. I couldn't believe it. I didn't want to believe it. And then, the unimaginable happened. More quickly than anyone could react, we heard the sound of a gun firing.

"I asked nicely. I'm done waiting," my dad said.

He had shot Chelsea square in the chest. She died instantly, and crumpled down to the ground. My dad—no, not my dad, Lucas—crouched down to pick up the memory block.

I could hear Rupert crying out for Chelsea. I thought I saw Samuel run towards them, but I couldn't really make out what I was seeing through my blurred vision. I tried to focus and pay attention to what was going on, but it was too hard.

I felt weak, and my heart rate was accelerating. My chest hurt. All of a sudden, my body ached more than it ever had before. I just wanted it all to stop. And just like that, everything turned black.

Chapter 30

When I came to, I was lying on the bed in Rupert's safe room. At first I didn't remember anything that had happened. And then, just like that, it all came flooding back into my mind.

Sarah and Samuel were packing a bunch of bags. They were stuffing in books, food, water pills, clothes...almost anything within sight. I looked around the room, but I couldn't see Rupert.

"Oh good, you're awake," Samuel said.

"Yeah, I guess," I replied.

"I'm sorry. I truly am. I had no idea."

"Neither did I," I responded.

Samuel filled me in on what had happened after I passed out. After Lucas shot and killed Chelsea, Samuel managed to wrestle him to the ground and knock the gun from his hands. Amanda fired at him, but missed. Rupert grabbed me and ran out of the building, with Samuel following closely behind.

As they were escaping the building, they could hear gun shots being fired nonstop. He didn't have to tell me the rest. I pretty much guessed that they killed all the other Grover State Rebellion members, as none of them were here with us.

"We need to go right now. Your parent—sorry, I mean Lucas and Amanda—know where this place is. They could be on their way right now. Or worse, the Grover State Police," Sarah said.

"Where do we go?" I asked. There was nowhere left to go.

"Back through the tunnel. Once we get to the other side, we'll hike as far as we have to until we're safe," she said.

Samuel handed me three large bags. I strapped them on to my body as best as I could, and waited for further direction.

Samuel opened the door in the floor that led into the hidden room.

"Rupert, we have to leave now," Samuel said, as he stuck his head through the opening.

After a few minutes, Rupert climbed back into the safe room holding Alexis tightly to his chest. Although his face was dry, I could tell he had been crying. His eyes were red, and his eyes were filled with sadness.

Samuel handed three bags to Rupert, and he

strapped them to his body. He had placed Alexis in a cloth contraption that allowed her to hang freely from his chest, leaving his hands free. That didn't matter though, because he clutched onto her like he was afraid of losing her.

Samuel led everyone outside and we made our way to the low priority neighbourhood. Everyone walked in silence. I think we were all just too sad to speak. Chelsea's death was fresh on everyone's mind.

When we arrived close to the low priority housing blocks, Samuel signalled for us to stop walking. We all ducked behind a row of bushes, and took in the scene before us.

The housing blocks were surrounded by police vehicles. There was no way we'd be going back home through that tunnel.

"What do we do?" Samuel asked.

"I don't know, but we need to leave the state as soon as possible. The longer we stay here, the longer we risk being captured," Sarah said.

"Come on, let's go," Rupert said.

Keeping low to the ground, we followed Rupert as we headed back, retracing our steps. I didn't know where we were going, but it was better than staying where we were.

We followed Rupert as he dodged from building to building, sticking to shadows. When we finally stopped, I realized we were standing in a car depot.

The car depot was where all state cars were kept. Drivers would pick up a car from the depot at the start of their shifts, and then park them back here before heading home.

Rupert walked to a car and pulled the door open. He motioned us to get inside with him. I was reluctant, but didn't really have any other options to offer. I got into the back seat, and Samuel got in beside me. Sarah got into the passenger seat beside Rupert.

"Rupert, what are we doing? As soon as we turn on the car, they're going to know where we are," Sarah said.

"Just wait," he said.

Rupert removed Alexis from the contraption on his chest, and handed her to Sarah. He removed something from his pocket that looked like a little black box, and reached below the seat. After a few minutes, I heard a loud pop as he removed a circular object that had been under the seat.

"What's that?" I asked.

"This is a chip bay. It's what allows them to monitor cars. It's where the p-chip is located. Without it, they won't be able to monitor our movement. Well, at least not electronically," he said.

Rupert opened the door and threw out the chip bay. He fiddled with something else below his seat, and then the car roared to life.

"Are you sure this is safe?" Samuel asked.

"Do you have any other options you care to share with the group?" Rupert retorted.

When Samuel remained quiet, Rupert turned off all the lights and started driving. At first I was sure that the police would be surrounding us within a matter of seconds. After we had been driving without incident for an hour, I started relaxing.

"Where exactly are we going?" I asked.

"To the border," Rupert replied.

"And then?"

"I guess we'll just have to see," he said.

I wasn't too happy with his response, but at least we'd be outside of the border, figuring out what to do.

Chapter 31

I was on alert the entire time we were driving, ready for the worst case scenario to present itself. Sarah was holding tightly onto Alexis, shielding her in case we were ambushed and caught by surprise. In the back seat beside me, Samuel had two guns at the ready on his lap.

I didn't recognize where we were at all. It had been a few hours since the last time I had seen a housing block. We saw a building every so often, but I couldn't recognize what they were. Based on how long we had been driving for, I assumed that they were military installations.

"How long until we get to the border?" Samuel asked.

"It shouldn't be too long now. About twenty minutes," Rupert replied.

"That close?" I asked.

"Yes. Once the paved road ends, we will be out of Grover State," he said.

"Then why didn't we just take this route all along. No one's following us. It seems a lot easier and safer than going into the city and through the sewers," I said.

"It's not," Rupert said. "Safer, that is. The borders are usually heavily patrolled by military soldiers."

The manor and candour of his response left us all in disbelief. At first I didn't think I properly understood what he had said. But when I noticed the same stunned look on Sarah and Samuel's faces, I knew that I had heard correctly.

"So, you're basically just driving us through a trap?" Sarah said.

"Did you have any other options? If you do, I'm all ears. This is the only option we have. Either we make it, or we don't. Let's try to make sure we don't see what happens if we get caught," Rupert said.

Everyone remained silent, and I saw Sarah clutch Alexis even closer to her chest. She lay a kiss on her forehead, and turned around to address me.

"Do you mind holding onto Alexis? Just make sure that she's not visible through the window," she said.

As she handed me Alexis, I noticed Samuel rummaging through his bag. He removed a small black blanket, and spread it around me and Alexis.

"Make sure you both stay under the cover," he said.

"Why? Won't they still be able to see me through the window? It seems rather obvious," I said.

"It's bulletproof," Sarah said. "Don't move it around. It should protect you. If anything happens..." She didn't finish her thought.

"What about you guys?" I asked. "Can't we just drive through them while wearing a bulletproof blanket?"

"No, we just have the one," Samuel said.

Samuel passed two guns to Sarah, a long one and a short one, and they both rolled down their windows. They both stuck the end of their guns out of their windows, and waited. There were now two guns aimed out of the right side of the car.

All of a sudden, Samuel wound his window back up, and stood up as much as the back seat would allow him.

"Switch spots with me," he said.

I pulled my legs onto the seat to allow him more room to pass, and scooted over to his side of the car. Once we were both settled in, he wound down his window and stuck his gun out of it. There was now a gun protruding out of both sides of the vehicle.

"As soon as you spot someone, anyone, shoot. We can't have any of them follow us outside of the border. That would be the same as being captured right now. If we can take them all out, we should have enough time to put distance between us and the state, before reinforcements are sent out. Chances are, they're already on their way," Rupert said.

"Yes," I echoed. "Probably at the direction of Amada and Lucas. My parents."

I wasn't seeking pity when I said that, but it still was heart warming to have Samuel quickly hug me, and Sarah reach back from the front seat to pat my knee.

As we continued approaching the border, I ducked down in my seat as much as I could. I could still see out of the window, but my body was partially obstructed from vision to anyone looking into the car.

Everything happened before I even had a chance to realize what was going on. I heard a gun go off. At first I thought someone was shooting at us, but soon realized that Sarah had shot off her gun. I didn't see who she hit, but she seemed to have gotten someone, as I heard her say "one down".

After that, the next half hour was a flurry of

gunfire. I could see two soldiers shooting at us, approaching from the right. Samuel was able to shot both of them, before they got close enough to do any damage.

Sarah was shooting at four soldiers that had appeared on her side. She had managed to shoot three of them, but one of the soldiers was still eluding her. We had the advantage of being in a moving vehicle, but that didn't stop him from landing a few shots into the side of the car.

Most likely due to the shooting, Alexis was now wide awake and crying. At first I thought she was calming down, but then her cries increased in volume, until she was practically shrieking at the top of her lungs.

"Megan, are you okay? Is Alexis okay?" Rupert asked from the driver's seat.

"Yes, we're fine," I replied.

I cradled Alexis tightly against my chest, and tried to shield her ears from the noise. It couldn't be too pleasant for her right now. I just imagined hearing this flurry of noise, and not knowing what was going on.

When I returned my attention to the window, I wasn't prepared for what I was seeing. There were at least ten soldiers running after us, shooting at the car. And this was only on the right side, where Sarah was shooting. I was too terrified to turn my head and see how many where on Samuel's side.

I closed my eyes tightly, and tried to focus on my breathing. I could feel myself getting light headed, and the last thing I needed was to pass out again. I couldn't afford to do that right now. I had to remain alert, to protect Alexis and provide any assistance I could to the others. If they had to take care of me as well, it could very well be the end for all of us.

My eyes remained closed as I heard shot after shot being fired from Sarah and Samuel's guns. I heard Sarah reloading, followed by a flurry of quick gunfire. I felt the passenger side door vibrate, as something hit it with a lot of force.

"Sam, to you right, ahead of us!" I heard Rupert yelling to Samuel. This was followed by rapid gunfire.

"Go faster! Faster!" Samuel bellowed from beside me.

My body lurched forward as the car was brought close to its maximum speed limit. As we bounced around in the backseat, Alexis continued crying. Her cries were muffled by the multiple shots being fired off at any given moment.

My eyes were still firmly closed when I felt the car come to a complete stop. I expected to hear more gun shots, but none came. I slowly opened my eyes and looked around. There was no one else within sight outside of the vehicle.

"Did we pass the border?" I asked no one in particular.

"Yes, we sure did," Sarah said.

Although the shootout had stopped, my ears were still ringing from the loud noise we had just been subjected to. Alexis was still crying, but her cry wasn't as piercing as before.

"Shouldn't we continue, you know, driving?" I asked Rupert.

We were stopped in the middle of nowhere, near Grover State Military soldiers that we had just killed. There were no doubt plenty more on the way. We couldn't afford to just sit here until they arrived.

"No, we ditch the car here," Rupert said. "I drove far enough to temporarily throw them off of our scent. We walk from here on out."

Both Sarah and Samuel were replacing their guns in their bags. Everyone had a gun tucked into their waistband, including myself, so the big weapons didn't need to be brought out until we needed them.

As we all got out of the car, Rupert immediately took Alexis from my arms and hugged her tightly. He turned himself to the side so that no one could see his face, but I could see a few trails of tears coming down the side of his cheeks.

"Are we ready to go?" Sarah asked.

Everyone nodded yes. Sarah placed her bag on the ground near my feet, and went back into the car. She ducked down under the front seat, so no one could see what she was doing. When she walked back towards us, she directed us to stand further away from the vehicle.

"Should we start heading out now?" Samuel asked.

"In a minute," Sarah responded.

None of us knew what we were waiting for, except for Sarah. I was growing a bit impatient myself, and the weight of the bags started to bear down on me since we weren't moving.

All of a sudden, I heard an explosion. The car burst into flames, and lay burning before our eyes. I watched as flames reached high into the sky, stretching out until they tapered off in a line of smoke.

"Okay, we can go now," Sarah said, as she picked up her bags and led the way.

We were now walking across an open field, but there was a forest visible in the short distance. Following Sarah, we walked towards the forest.

Chapter 32

We had been hiking through the forest for hours. None of us knew exactly what time it was, but dawn had crept up upon us without any of us realizing it, and it was now bright and shiny outside.

From our current position, we could no longer see the smoke coming from the burning car. I was starting to get tired, but everyone else seemed full of energy. I didn't say anything, because I didn't want them to view me as weak. I wanted them to view me equal to them.

It wasn't until a few hours later that we finally stopped to set up camp. Samuel had a tent in his bag, and he set it up with Sarah. Rupert handed me Alexis, and said that he was going to gather some firewood.

"Rupert, wait!" I called out after him, just before he disappeared between two trees. "Can I help too, I asked?"

I was tired of never contributing. I was tired of being treated like a helpless child, just as Alexis was. At least Alexis was a baby and truly needed the babying. There was no reason for me to not be able to help.

"Sure, why not," he said to me. Directing his attention to Samuel and Sarah, he said to them, "Do you mind watching over Alexis, while we gather some firewood?"

"Sure," Samuel said, as he took Alexis from my arms.

I followed Rupert as we began our search for firewood. I was in charge of collecting small dry branches, and Rupert was in charge of the larger ones. It wasn't really that hard to do; it just required a lot of bending. Once we both had a fairly substantial pile, we made our way back towards our camp.

"Wait a second," Rupert said.

He stopped in his tracks, and bent down over a row of shrubs. I watched as he picked up a few flowers very delicately. I waited silently until he was finished, and followed him back to camp.

When we arrived back at camp, Sarah and Samuel had finished putting up the tent. While we were gone, one of them had gone out to forage, because there was a small collections of berries on the floor.

I helped Rupert set up the fire. I wasn't too sure how to build one, but found that it was pretty easy. I just did as Rupert directed, and before shortly, we had a beautiful blaze in front of us.

We got out a few tubes of MGNS and a bottle of water pills, enough for everyone. I helped Rupert arrange a few logs around the fire, so that we could all have somewhere to sit down.

"Guys, do you mind coming for a minute?" Rupert called out to Sarah and Samuel.

Both of them came to join us, with Alexis in tow. Samuel handed Alexis over to Rupert, and took a seat on one of the logs. I handed out a tube of MGNS to everyone, and passed around the bottle of water pills.

Rupert arranged Alexis' clothing so that it was neat and straight. Cradling her in one arm, he picked up the flowers that he had picked. He slowly handed one to everyone, and we all took the flowers offered in silence.

No one spoke for a while, because no one dared to interrupt the silence. Rupert was feeding Alexis, but had neglected to eat himself. Finally, once Alexis was full, he addressed us.

"If you don't mind, I just thought we could..." He wasn't able to finish his sentence. A few tears started streaming down his eyes.

"Sure, buddy. We would love to," Samuel said.

I wasn't sure what they were referring to, and I didn't understand how Samuel knew exactly what he was talking about. I looked at Sarah, hoping that she would ask them what they were referring to. Unfortunately, not only did she not ask, but she seemed to understand what they were talking about as well. Not too sure what to do, I observed in silence.

"Do you want to go first?" Sarah asked Rupert.

"No, I want to go last," he said.

"I'll go first," Sarah said. "I miss Chelsea. I miss her so much. Even though I was there, it doesn't seem real. She didn't deserve that. She was my best friend. She's the reason why I joined the rebellion. I miss her so much. I love you, Chelsea."

She dropped her flower into the fire, and we all watched as it withered and turned black. Samuel was the next to speak.

"Chelsea was...what can I say? She was amazing. She was also the reason I joined the rebellion. I remember her fondly. She was a true friend. A good friend, a good mother, a good person. I will miss you, Chelsea. I love you," he said.

He dropped his flower into the fire, and we

watched it burn. As we were once more enveloped in silence, I realized that it was my turn to speak. I wasn't sure what to say. What could I say?

"Chelsea was... Chelsea was one of the only friends I've ever had, with the exception of you three. She was nice to me. She cared for me. For no reason whatsoever, she made me family," I said. "I'm really sad that she's gone. She deserves to be sitting here more than I do."

"Don't say that," Sarah said. "Your life is just as valuable."

I dropped my flower in the fire, and watched as it burned above the ashes of the other two. It was now Rupert's turn. He was holding two flowers in his hands: one for him, and one for Alexis. Tears started streaming down his face before he spoke.

"Chelsea, I miss you. I miss you so much. You should be the one standing here with Alexis, not me. You're smarter, stronger, and everything better than me. You didn't deserve this. I... I didn't know. I should have known something was amiss. I should have protected you. I should have been the one to...

"I miss you, Chelsea. Alexis misses you too. She's been crying a lot more lately. She knows that her mom is gone. I promise you that I will protect her

263

until my dying breathe. And I promise, she will never forget you. I will never forget you. I love you, Chelsea. I miss you so much," Rupert said.

He delicately dropped both flowers into the fire, and we all watched in silence as they too burned. After a few minutes, he grabbed a pile of flowers that had previously been hidden from sight. Dropping the flowers one by one into the fire, he dedicated each one to the other fallen members of the Grover State Rebellion.

Everyone remained quiet for the remainder of the day. At one point, I helped Sarah place all of our bags in the tent. With the help of Samuel, we also set up a watch post. We placed three guns inside of the tent within arm's reach, just in case anything happened while we were sleeping.

"Are you sure they won't find us while we're sleeping?" Samuel asked.

"I think we've hiked far enough," Sarah replied. "I don't think we should be running into them any time soon. At least, I hope we don't."

"Who's taking the first post?" Rupert asked.

"I'll take it," I said.

At first, I was expecting everyone to protest, and say that I should just sleep in the tent and not worry myself. Surprisingly, no words of protest came. Instead, Samuel ducked into the tent, retrieved a gun, and handed it to me.

"I'll take the second shift," he said. "Wake me up when you think a few hours have gone by."

As a smile spread across my face, despite all the unpleasantness of our current situation, I grabbed the gun from him. I placed it near the watch post, not wanting to accidentally set it off.

Rupert spread a blanket on the floor, and invited everyone to come lay down on it. We all laid down on the blanket, looking up at the sky. We didn't have to wait much longer to see the sun set.

After a while, everyone started going into the tent to sleep. I was left lying on the blanket alone with only Sarah for company, but I heard her get up as well.

"Are you going to be okay?" she asked.

"Yes, I'll be fine," I replied.

She smiled and nodded, and gave me a quick hug. I watched her disappear into the tent, and then zip up the enclosure. Left alone, I sat down at the watch post, gun in hand.

Chapter 33

When I woke up the next morning, I was in the tent sandwiched between Samuel and Sarah. The night before, I had stayed up keeping watch until I had difficulty keeping my eyes open. I woke up Samuel as he had directed, and we switched spots. As he settled into the watch post we had built, I fell asleep as soon as my head hit the ground inside the tent.

For breakfast, we ate the berries that had been collected the day before, along with some MGNS. I helped Samuel put away the tent, and pack everything else up.

"Where are we headed now?" I asked.

"I guess we'll continue hiking until we're a hundred percent out of Grover State territory. I can't promise you for certain, but I'm sure that we'll eventually come across civilization. The real word," Rupert said.

"How long until we get there?" I asked.

"If we get there, maybe a couple of weeks. Or a couple of months. I can't really say," he responded.

Once everything was packed up and we were

ready to leave, Rupert strapped Alexis into the contraption on his chest and we set off deeper into the forest.

*****

We had been hiking for most of the day, only stopping quickly for short rest breaks. The sky was getting darker, and we were all growing tired. Rupert was still leading us, and we followed him in silence.

"Everyone, quiet!" Rupert quietly exclaimed, stopping in his tracks.

I stopped behind Sarah as I heard Samuel stopping behind me. I looked around by I couldn't spot what had gotten a hold of Rupert's attention.

All of a sudden, I heard a branch break under someone's feet. Everyone else seemed to have heard it to, because I suddenly felt myself being pushed down to the ground by Samuel. Peering under his arms, I tried to look for the offending party.

"Meg, do you have your gun?" Samuel whispered in my ear.

"Yes," I whispered, as I nodded at the same time.

"Stay with Sarah. I'm going to go cover Rupert; he has Alexis," he said, as I felt him getting up.

"Do you know who made that noise? Is it a Grover State soldier?" I asked.

Samuel must not have heard me, because I didn't get a response. I slowly got up, and saw Sarah behind me. Pulling out my gun from my waistband, I went to go stand beside her. I tried to remove the safety as silently as I could, and aimed it in front of me. Whatever the noise was, it appeared to be coming from in front of us.

"Don't shoot!" A voice shouted from ahead of us, still hidden by the forest.

At the same time, we all aimed our guns slightly to the right, in the direction that the voice was coming from. We heard a few more branches break, and then a figure emerged from behind a tree.

The man that emerged was clothed in black from head to toe, and was wearing a hat on his head. Although he was armed, his gun was still visibility hanging at his side. As he saw all four of us with guns aimed at him, he raised his hands over his head.

"Don't shoot," he said again.

"Who are you? What are you doing here?" Samuel asked him.

I wasn't sure what to make of him. He wasn't wearing a Grover State military or police uniform.

Although the clothes he was wearing wasn't necessarily odd, no one in Grover State dressed in all black.

"My name is Randall Hart. I was flying overhead when I saw a huge fire down below. I thought it was a distress signal, so I landed my plane close by. When I didn't find anyone near the wreck, I decided to walk around for a bit to see if I could find someone. And now, it appears that I have."

I could see the hesitation in Samuel. Although his gun was still aimed at Randall, it had been lowered and his demeanour had changed.

"You're not from Grover State?" Samuel asked him.

"Grover State? Sorry, I don't know what that is," he replied.

"You're not military? Police?"

"Military? No. I'm just a pilot, on my way home," he replied.

"Where's home? Where are you from?" Rupert piped in.

"Canada," he responded.

I remembered reading about Canada in one of Rupert's books. I also remembered seeing it pictured in the safe room in Amber and Tammy's unit. Based on the map, if I remembered correctly, Canada was attached to the country that used to be here, until Grover State took over. I couldn't quite remember the name, but I was sure I was right.

"You're from Canada?" Sarah asked him. "Why are you flying here?"

"It's the same route I always take. I'm a pilot. I fly. Usually, in the sky," he said.

"Don't move," Samuel said. He approached Randall and took the gun that was hanging at his side. "Do you have any other weapons?" When he shook his head no, Samuel took a few steps back.

"If you try anything, I'm going to shoot you," Samuel said.

"Sounds fair," Randall replied.

"Everyone, guns down," Samuel directed.

I put the safety back on my gun, and placed it back in my waistband. I noticed Rupert and Sarah doing the same, but Samuel still had his gun out. Randall slowly lowered his arms, and walked towards us. Samuel kept his gun trained on him, until he sat down on a log and leaned back.

"So, do you guys need a lift," Randall asked.

"Are you serious?" Sarah asked. "You'd bring us with you?"

"Sure, no problem. You all seem to be in distress. That was kind of the point of me landing my plane, you know. If you want, we can head to my plane right now, and take off at sunrise," he said.

"Rupert, what do you think?" Sarah asked him.

"It's worth a shot," he replied.

"Megan, what about you?" she asked me.

I was completely taken off guard with her inclusion of my opinion, but I quickly recovered. "I guess it seems okay."

"Sam?" she asked.

"Sure, why not," he replied.

"Lead the way," Sarah told him.

We all followed Randall, retracing our steps. I was trying to contain the excitement in my heart. We were so close to being saved, I could almost taste it. But there was also a nagging feeling in the back of my mind that thought this might all just be a trap.

Chapter 34

We were all tired beyond belief, but no one wanted to stop to take a break. We were all eager to get back to Randall's plane, and get out of here.

Samuel was still sceptical of him. He had his gun loosely trained on his back, and said that he wouldn't believe a word of what Randall had said, until he saw the plane with his own two eyes.

As we continued hiking through the forest, I noticed that it was noticeably getting brighter ahead of us. We were approaching the clearing that we had entered from. We were almost there.

As we exited the forest, the first thing I saw was the charred remains of the car. It was burnt to a crisp, and had burnt the ground surrounding it. As I turned my head to the left, I noticed an airplane. Randall hadn't been lying.

"I'm sorry I doubted you," Samuel said, as he placed his gun back into his waistband. "I just had to be sure. We've been through a lot. We couldn't take any chances."

"Understood. I guess it's a good thing I found

you guys," he replied. "What exactly are you guys hiding from, if I may ask?"

"That's a story for another time," Samuel said.

"Megan, help me set up camp," Sarah said to me.

I obliged, and helped her get the tent out of Samuel's bag. It seemed really complicated at first, but we had the tent up in no time. After a lot of back and forth, everyone agreed that Randall could sleep in the tent with us. Since we wouldn't be sleeping for that long, Samuel offered to keep post for the entire night. He said that he could just sleep in the plane, once we took off tomorrow morning.

Laying down in the tent was really awkward. I was squished between Randall and Rupert. Sarah was on Randall's other side, and Alexis was sleeping in Rupert's arms. I tried to fall asleep, but I found it hard. My veins were coursing with adrenaline, and I remained wide awake.

By now, everyone else had fallen asleep. Samuel had built a fire outside, and I could see the flames of the fire projected as shadows on the tent. I stared at it, hoping that it would lull me to sleep. It didn't.

I tried closing my eyes, hoping that my body

would be duped into sleep. When that didn't help, I turned to my side, and stared at Alexis. She looked so peaceful, sleeping serenely in Rupert's arms.

After a while of laying on my side, my arm started to hurt. I shifted my body so that I was now lying on the opposite side, and facing Randall's sleeping body.

Randall slept with his mouth open, and had a light snore that would sound intermittently. I studied him as he lay lying before me. Now that his hat was removed, I noticed that he had short brown hair, cropped close to his face. He had stubble on his chin and cheeks, and his teeth were a dark shade of white.

As I continued studying his features, I noticed that there was something on his left wrist. I couldn't quite tell what it was, as his sleeve covered most of it. My curiosity got the best of me, as I carefully lifted his sleeve up to see what it was. As soon as I did, my mouth fell agape.

Untangling myself from my blankets as quickly as I could, I ran out of the tent. I guess my commotion had woken up Rupert, because he wiped his eyes and opened them. When he did, they landed on me zipping the tent open.

"Megan? Are you okay?" he asked. His voice

was groggy from sleep.

"Yes," I whispered. "I just need to urinate."

He must have accepted my response at face value, because he was back to being fast asleep by the time I was outside of the tent, and zipping it closed.

Samuel was sitting close to the tent, near the fire. His gun was lying delicately on his legs, ready to be used at a moment's notice.

"Samuel?" I asked.

"Hey kid. Need to pee?" he replied.

"There was something on Randall's wrist. I didn't know what... I was curious, so I... Randall has an identity chip," I whispered.

As soon as the words came out of my mouth, Samuel jumped up.

"Are you sure?" he asked me.

I nodded yes, and followed him as he walked towards the tent.

"What are you going to do?" I asked him.

"Kill him," he stated.

I watched as Samuel quietly unzipped the tent, holding his gun tight by his side. Aiming his gun at Randall's sleeping body, he kicked at Sarah's feet.

"Sarah, wake up," he whispered.

As Sarah slowly awoke from her sleep, her

eyes adjusted to her surroundings. As soon as she saw Samuel pointing a gun at Randall, she became wide awake.

"Check his wrist," Samuel whispered.

Sarah grabbed his left wrist, as it was the one closest to her. She slowly lowered his sleeve, and almost dropped his hand when she revealed his identity chip.

Without any further communication between Sarah and Samuel—at least, none that I could see—she took off her belt, and looped it around both of his hands. As soon as his hands were secured, Samuel placed his gun in his waistband, and grabbed a hold of his feet. Pulling with all his might, he dragged Randall out of the tent.

The commotion was enough to wake Randall up. As he awoke and noticed that his hands were bound, he started struggling.

"What the hell? What's going on? Why am I tied up?" he yelled out.

"You're a liar," Samuel said to him.

"Come on, what more do you want from me? I brought you to my plane, and offered you a free ride. My plane is literally only a few feet away from us. You're telling me that's not enough proof? Come on, untie my hands." Randall responded.

"What's that on your wrist?" Sarah asked him.

All of a sudden, his demeanour changed. His mouth changed from a friendly grin to a cold smirk. A small chuckle escaped his throat.

"Well then, I guess I'm found out," he said.

"You know I'm going to kill you, right?" Samuel said.

"Go ahead. You're all dead anyways. It's only a matter of time before they find you."

"But why?" Sarah asked. "Why pretend? Why not just kill us when you found us? Are you military? Police? Who are you, really?"

"I told you, I'm Randall Hart," he responded. He ignored all of her other questions.

All the noise we were making caused Rupert to wake up. He stumbled out of the tent with Alexis in tow, rubbing his eyes.

"Hey guys. Is it already sunrise? Are we—" Rupert stopped talking mid sentence, as he finally registered what was happening.

"Military or police?" he asked.

"We don't know. He has an identity chip though. There's no doubt that they already know our location, and are on their way here," Sarah said.

"Here, hold Alexis for me," he said, as he handed her to Sarah.

Rupert walked over to the plane, and disappeared inside. We had no idea what he was doing, and remained in our current positions. Randall was still on the ground, smirking and chuckling at our imminent peril.

"Can you please shut him up?" Samuel asked.

Sarah walked over to Randall and kicked him squarely in the head.

"Is he dead?" I asked.

"No, just unconscious. At most, he'll wake up with a well-deserved headache," she said.

We patiently waited until Rupert re-emerged from the plane. He was carrying two large boxes, which he promptly dropped on the floor near Randall's unconscious body.

"Okay, what are you waiting for? Let's go," he said.

"Go where, Rupert? Are you out of your mind? Where are we going to go that they won't find us? We don't have a car, we're on foot. I guarantee you they'll have cars. It'll only be a matter of time before they catch up with us," Samuel said.

"I think you misunderstood me. We're not

going back into the forest, on foot. We're going into the air, in that," he said, as he pointed to the plane. "I took out anything that they could use to track us with."

"Well, that's a brilliant idea there, Rupert. Well, except for the fact that none of us knows how to pilot a plane. Would you happen to have a Plan B up your sleeve?" Samuel retorted.

"I can fly it," Rupert replied.

"Are you sure?" Sarah interjected.

"Yes," he replied.

Without another word, we all set about to dismantle the tent and place all of our things inside of the plane. Once we were all inside, Rupert closed the door.

The plane had ten plush seats, more than enough for us to be comfortable the entire journey. There was small fridge loaded with MGSN and small bottles of liquid. As I looked around, I saw Grover State's logo prominently displayed on one of the walls.

"So, what do we do now?" I asked.

Cradling Alexis close to his chest, Rupert took a second to look into each of our eyes. "First, we fly this plane out of here. There should be enough fuel to get us far away from here. Once we land, we will rest. Once we're officially out of Grover State, we will recruit help from the outside world. Then, we will train. And then, we come back."

We all sat in silence, as we let Rupert's words sink in. He handed Alexis over to Sarah, and disappeared into the cockpit.

"Do you have a marker?" I asked Sarah and Samuel.

Samuel quickly fetched a marker out of his bag and handed it to me. Uncapping the marker, I went to stand across the state's logo, until I could touch it. With careful and deliberate strokes, I spelled out REBELLION beneath the Grover State emblem.